CHASING RORY

BOOK TWO OF THE LOVE WARS SERIES

MICHELLE MARS

This book is dedicated to my parents who instilled in me a travel bug as alive today as it was the day I chose to start my college experience by living in Sevilla, located in Andalusia, the southern region of Spain. They taught me to embrace cultures not just tour them. To fall in love with what makes us all unique. That each culture has its own rhythm, food, music, art, dress, and dance. I've been falling in love with the diversity of our planet ever since. Sevilla was the first time I did so as an adult and on my own.

To my late father (miss you every day) and to my Mom (my friend and travel partner), thank you for teaching me to appreciate the world for the gorgeous tapestry that it is. In my writing, I will always aim to reflect the beauty I've been so privileged to see.

I love you beyond words.

AUTHOR'S NOTE

Dear Reader,

What can I say?

While studying abroad in Sevilla, I fell in love. Not with an alien, because I haven't met any yet and definitely not hunky warrior ones. No. I fell in love with Andalusia. The people, the food, the culture, the music, the clothes, and so much more. There was so much warmth. So much love for life. So much community. Even if they could be found having a yelling match on a street corner regarding whether churros is traditional or if it is only traditional if it is churros con chocolate. I'm firmly team con chocolate in case you're wondering.

There is no way to really talk about Andalusian culture, though, without discussing the Gitano people. They are a segment of the broader Romani community that settled into southern Spain and their influence on Andalusia can be seen everywhere. The Gitano community, as with many of the Romani, have been discriminated against and often shunned in the societies they traveled through or settled into.

In Andalusia, while that was still true, it was also true that the cultures ended up blending. That blending birthed Flamenco as we know it today, as an example. Flamenco is both the dance and the music and it was not uncommon to walk along the street and see a group of people start clapping, singing, and dancing just to pass the afternoon. Flamenco is storytelling. It is art. It is expression. It is emotional. It is connection.

Chasing Rory is also about connection and coming together, and Rory came to be from my love and experiences from that time and place in my life.

I do not aim to tell the story of the Gitano people. That is not my story to tell. Their struggles, triumphs, challenges, and journeys are their own and you should read those stories from the authors who belong to that community and lived those experiences.

My goal as a romance author has and always will be to reflect the diversity that exists in our world and to give each character that speaks to me their agency, individuality, respect, and, of course, a happily ever after.

I fell in love with Rory's journey and I hope you do too.

Thank you for reading,

Michelle Mars

If Rory speaks to you, then I highly recommend doing more research through Gitano-run organizations. I've been personally inspired reading articles from the feminists in the Gitano community. Make sure to seek out books, poetry, and articles written by Gitano writers.

Breaking Earth News

World of News Times

We scour the internet so you don't have to.

To all our fellow humans, the following news has come from multiple sources within multiple governments. We have verified and reverified our verifications because this is a big deal and we wanted to be sure before we shared it.

All relocation off of Earth is now optional. You heard us correctly. The Alien Relocation Cooperative leaders, the Staraban; and our favorite mostly-peaceful resistance movement, the Humans Against Relocation Movement, have teamed up to prove whether Earth is really dying. Apparently, that has now come into question.

Sources tell us there is a third party involved, but they don't have any more details than that. Something definitely smells fishy and we will keep you informed with any new developments.

Foremost in our thoughts? What about those who have already been relocated? Will they be able to return?

Stay tuned to WONT for answers as they become available.

Phoenix Bordnow

WONT Senior Writer

[1]

ENCOUNTER AT KNIFE POINT

Captain's Log: Earth date October 9, 2025

The Staraban-alien-dumbass, also known as Bren, has decreed that little ol' human me is to stay put on Earth for my own safety. What this oversized, golden, hotness doesn't understand is that there is only one captain of my life and it sure as hell isn't him.

My newest friend and coconspirator, Jill, and I plan to stowaway aboard his ship if I can't convince him, one way or another, to relent. After all, I've only gotten where I am today because of my wit and cunning. Okay, and maybe my ruthlessness.

Whatever.

Don't judge.

Anyway… Hopefully he can be made to see reason because it's not just his ship I want to board and ride. The next captain's log will be made in space because that is the final frontier.

¡Nos vamos!

Rory out.

CHAPTER 1

Staraban Base, Northern California

October 9, 2025

Bren of the Staraban, fierce warrior and second-in-command of the Alien Relocation Cooperative (ARC), never cowered from anyone. The opposite. With his scarred face and tall muscular stature, he was feared by many across the known universe. Therefore, he had to ask himself how he had ended up in the predicament he was in at that moment. Actually, he knew. Two words. Aurora Espinoza. Ever since he met the diminutive, curvaceous, and sexy human female, nothing made much sense.

Rory with her thick, dark brown, wavy hair that he wanted to feel cascading around him as he held her close. Her big, expressive, yellow-green eyes that he wanted to see glazed in desire. Her warm, light brown skin that he wanted to see flushed and naked against his. Her full sensual mouth that he wanted to see wrapped around his—Bren flinched back to awareness as another knife sailed just past his thigh. The very lips he had imagined doing wicked things were currently yelling profanities at him in two Earth languages, as she continued her rather dangerous form of disagreement.

Rory, a munitions expert, which he had only learned about recently, was proficient with most weapons. He hoped with her perfect aim, she was missing him on purpose. She got really fucking close, though. Without turning to look, he could guess that there was a knife outline of him in his wall. Only *she* would come to have a conversation wielding throwing knives. It was hard to tell if her knives or her words could skewer with more painful impact.

"Rory, you are being unreasonable *and* homicidal." He realized his mistake too late because that was the wrong thing to say. Two more knives embedded in his wall. One had come uncomfortably close to his groin.

"I'm unreasonable? Me? ¡Cabrón!" She seemed to use that word a lot around him. "You haven't seen unreasonable. I'm going to go get something bigger to make my point. Don't move." She threw her last knife and this time it caught the slightest bit of his uniform pant leg, pinning it to the wall with an exclamatory thud. She turned and made her way to the exit.

He pulled his leg, hard, ripping his pant leg, and caught up to her just as she reached the door. He turned her around and pinned her to it with his hands on her shoulders. "I think not. Do I need to ask my brother to lock you up for my safety and yours? This is my decision and I will not endanger you by taking you on this mission. That is final. You do not understand the dangers that exist out in space and you are human."

"What does that mean?"

"It means that your species is very easy to kill."

Her eyes narrowed at him. "I have every right to come on this mission. The All Alien Alliance will be hearing and making judgements about events that were perpetrated against *my* planet. *My* people."

He reluctantly agreed that she had a point. They *had* learned the Vrolans had lied about Earth's dying-planet status. The deception was especially disturbing because they had hired his family's company, ARC, to move the humans to another planet. They needed to be reported to AAA to start an investigation. And, in most cases, a representative of the alien species impacted should be there.

But… They did not want to waste time waiting for the various Earth governments to assign a representative and there was no way he would be bringing her. So… point or not, she was not coming.

She continued to argue her case. "Some of my people should be present for this. *You* are being unreasonable. I can defend myself, as the knives in your wall can attest."

"The fact that I now have you pinned to my door and at my mercy says differently. One wrong mo—" He groaned, his dual hearts beating harder, and her name came out as a plea. "Rory." He laid his forehead down on the top of her head. She was so small. So delicate. She had him completely at her mercy, and she knew it. "What are you doing?"

"I would've thought it was obvious. I could've sworn that I'd heard you had a lot of experience with the opposite sex." She continued to rub her hand slowly up and down his ever growing shaft.

"You heard wrong."

"Did I?"

"I have had a lot of experience with everyone."

"We have that in common then."

His breath caught as she squeezed. Her hand was so small and yet she applied just the right amount of pressure to drive him wild. He wanted so much more. He wanted to feel her hand on his actual cock with no material separating them.

"Rory. You keep that up, and you will see exactly how much knowledge I have. I will make you feel so good. Let me pleasure you."

"You want to bring me pleasure?" Her voice dripped with sex just like his cock was doing.

"Yes. So much pleasure." His hips pushed forward even more fully into her hand. He moved one hand from her shoulder to cup her cheek and turn her face up to his. She looked him in the eyes with a small smile playing along her lips.

"If you really want to give me pleasure—" She paused and bit her bottom lip drawing his eyes and all of his attention to the spot. He was so riveted, that he almost missed her next words, and then his brain registered what she said. "—then I need your respect. Being respected gives me pleasure. Let me come with you on this mission."

He looked back into her eyes and saw the steel there. The resolve. The pride. And everything came back into focus. She was using sex as a weapon. Seducing him to get her way. He wanted this one human more than he could ever remember wanting anyone else, and all she wanted was to come on his mission. His once over-heated blood turned to ice. "No."

He stepped away from her. One step. Two steps. Three. Until he could breathe. Until he could gather his composure.

"You will *not* be coming. I have a lot of preparations to complete and do not have time for your type of *negotiations*." He saw her flinch and hated himself a bit for hurting her.

"Woooow. On Earth mere months and already catching on to harmful stereotypes. Impressive. I tell you that I want to be respected for the independent woman that I am, treated as an equal, and all you see is a woman manipulating you. Well, fuck you."

He was so angry at the idea that she had just been using his desire for her against him, that he did not process whatever else she had just said. Though, it was hard to miss her parting shot of "Fuck you." Yep. Fuck him. He had a mission to get back to planning and did not have time for her manipulations.

Because if he had the time, he would have to admit it hurt that her seduction only happened for ulterior motives.

Because if he had the time, he would have to admit he had wanted her since the moment they met.

Six Days Earlier...

Bren could not believe he had allowed the human male to take him prisoner. Under normal circumstances, he would have been able to kill him within minutes, but these had not been normal circumstances. He had not been aiming to kill him. He had the feeling that choosing to kill him would make matters much, much worse on Earth as well as between his brother and the female he was lusting after. Even without taking the female into account, they had come to Earth on a peaceful mission to save the humans from their dying planet by relocating them to another one. They had even found them a new planet and thought it would be an easy job. That was what his family's company excelled at, after all. ARC took commissions across the universe from aliens needing a new place to live. They would send their scientists to find a compatible planet and then relocation would commence.

That was how it was supposed to work.

But on Earth they had encountered a lot of resistance. Of course, humans were not the ones that commissioned ARC this time and on top of that, humans were primitive in their exploration of space and had not been prepared to find out they were not alone in the universe at the same time as needing to be relocated. He still thought it showed rather poor judgement for them to be so resistant to being saved, but try explaining that to humans. In an attempt to make it as easy for them as possible, Bren had even worked with ARC's alien relations group to create a pamphlet that should have answered all the questions that humans might have had. That had been completely unsuccessful. Resistance movements had popped up everywhere, which made a non-violent relocation that much more challenging.

Now they were leading him through the Humans Against Relocation Movement base. A prisoner. Embarrassing. They entered an office and Bren wanted to growl as he was deposited in a chair against the wall. This was not a role he was used to playing.

Will, his captor, paced the small space, appearing deep in thought. The tall, dark-skinned human was clearly agitated. The door opened and Bren jumped to his feet, breaking the arms off of the wooden chair, and mentally tensing even as his body relaxed in preparation to address a potential new threat. He was not prepared.

A tiny beauty walked over and got right into his space. *Fash* she smelled good. Her scent whispered along his skin making his senses go wild. If she was going to be his guard, he was ready to be their prisoner. He pictured leaning down and taking her mouth. He bet her lips would be soft and pliant under his. He swayed forward just a bit, lost in his sensual musings.

"¿Dónde está mi amiga?"

Her tone of voice penetrated his imaginings and it finally registered that she was glaring up at him. Looking more ready to kill than kiss. Staraban warriors had a heightened sense of smell that had developed as a tool for tracking and fighting. The only things radiating from her were her intoxicating personal scent and the almost burning scent of pure fury.

Thinking of this little human coming up to him in a threatening manner had an unplanned smile splay across his face. It was one of his well-practiced and galaxy-tested seductive smiles, one that had gotten him almost anyone he ever wanted to enthusiastically jump into his bed. Maybe if he was not as intoxicated with her as he was, he would have noticed the right hook heading directly for his chin.

Rory had arrived at Will's office full of anxiety and anger. The anxiety was in wanting to know that her best friend, Jack, was okay. But her anger was far and away much more potent. It felt uncontainable. She was mad at everyone, but mostly she was devastatingly angry with herself. She was a hundred percent sure that she was the last person who had any interaction with Jack before she was kidnapped. When Jack hadn't answered the door at Rory's knock, she should have known something was off. Her instincts tried to warn her at the time, but other instincts had taken over and she had allowed her friend to get kidnapped. Being around Jack when she was so turned on for days in a row had affected Rory's own libido on a biological level so she'd left to play nurse with the new doctor assigned to their base.

As soon as she'd heard about Will taking a prisoner, she'd rushed over. It may not be fair to take all of her anger out on one alien, and the wrong one at that, but really, fuck it. She needed an outlet and he was going to prove useful. She opened the door ready to torture, kill, or maim whoever was there until she got Jack back.

She strode in and her heart stuttered. The most beautiful, fierce, and totally should-be-off-limits, golden god-of-a-guy was sitting handcuffed to a chair he dwarfed. As soon as she entered, he stood, easily breaking through the arms of the chair he'd been ridiculously attached to, and holy hell, he was tall and all muscle. Her anger at herself doubled at lusting for her enemy. She could not allow her libido free rein. Jack needed her and she was the shitty friend having the insta-hots for an alien she should see as just a means to getting Jack back.

She put all lustful thoughts on full lockdown and walked right up to the asshole. Surely he was an asshole. He had to be. As she yelled at him, he had the audacity to turn a seductive smile on her instead of answering her question and a few things happened all at once. She became aware of how damn good he smelled. So good, her mouth watered. Which made her instantly angrier. In a subconscious response to all that brewing anger, her punch connected with his face before she even thought to hit him.

"Fuck." Her knuckles hurt from the direct hit, but, damn, she finally felt a little better. Braced for any retaliation, she relaxed when she heard the steady rhythm of his hearts.

She'd always been a tad bit aggressive. She wasn't proud of it and it wasn't often that others saw that side of her, but as a panther shifter, Rory was a predator. There would always be a part of her that was primal. The only person who knew about her was Jack and since Jack was a vampire, they kept each other's secrets.

The alien grimaced after she hit him and yelled some alien word that she assumed was a lot like fuck or damn or perhaps they had one word that means, "I'm going to kill you when I get the chance." Whatever. She didn't need to know. What she did need to know was information about Jack. "I asked you about Jack. I want a fucking answer. What is your leader doing to her?"

The smile was back on his stupid, gorgeous face, "I believe they are doing it together."

"Rory!" Will yelled her name from near his desk. "Please don't kill my bargaining piece. I understand the desire, but I need you to show restraint."

She whirled on Will. "How could you leave her there? What happened?"

Will ran a hand over his bald held and down over his face. "I'm sorry. I almost had her out and then Tarc tackled her and this one —" Will waved his hand at the alien, "and I started fighting and let's just say it was a shit show. The only thing I could think to do was take a hostage so we could initiate a prisoner exchange. Apparently, I'm out of practice from my special forces days. Of course, then I had a team." He shook his head, as though clearing his thoughts, and continued, "What you need to know is that I'll get her back. I have someone calling the main Alien communication line as we speak."

She nodded her head just as the sound of Will's assistant came over the line. "I have the main office and they are putting you through to the alien you requested. Transferring the call to your phone now."

In the background she heard an angry male voice over the speaker yelling about his brother. So. This was Tarc's brother. Even better. She wondered if the aliens had balls, like human men, and if cutting them off would be the right thing to threaten him with. Only one way to find out.

A while later, Bren was quite sure that human females had something about them that made his species lose all common sense because he could not get Rory out of his head and what kind of masochist was he to want to get intimate with the woman threatening to cut his balls off? He also could not believe that Tarc leaving him with the rebels instead of trading him for his female. What kind of magical pussy powers did these females wield? He had been in a cell under heavy guard ever since the phone call with Tarc. Each side promised no harm would come to their prisoner. Well, except Rory, she did not seem ready to promise anything. He was not overly concerned, he could handle himself. Also, his brother had escaped his captivity here quite easily.

Her scent wafted to him seconds before she stood in the doorway, glaring. Her look was at odds with the scent of arousal he was getting off of her.

"So. Bren, against my suggestions, we will not be torturing you… yet. Instead, I've been instructed to keep you well guarded but otherwise allow you to join us at the dining hall. If you're hungry, then vamos." Just like that, she turned and headed out the door.

He was always hungry and it would be a good idea to learn the layout of the base, so he followed her, passing a pair of unhappy guards on his way out. Clearly, they were on the side of torture.

Bren followed her up some stairs and down a nondescript hall. From one of the rooms he could hear voices raised. He thought he made out Will's raised voice and then someone else yelling back something about rushing in without a plan or backup. If they were talking about Will's ridiculous one-man attempt at a rescue, then he had to agree. You have to properly plan for a rescue, not just rush in. There was more yelling and something about needing to be a savior but by then they had gotten too far away to hear more. He did hear Rory mumbling under her breath, but she stopped almost as soon as she started. He could have sworn it had something to do with assholes and men.

After too many hallways and turns, they reached a big open room. Instantly, he was steeped in the scent of the human food on offer and his mouth began watering. They walked silently toward one corner where there was a kitchen with a food serving area in front. The closer they got, the stronger the scent, the more distracted he became.

At least until he took note of the way Rory transformed as she greeted those they passed. She responded with winks and humor and lightness. If he thought her stunningly beautiful before, he could not take his eyes off of her now.

A sexy female practically bounced up to Rory. She whispered to her even as Rory tucked a stray blue hair behind the other woman's ear. The intimacy of the gesture was obvious. They stood close together. Too close.

Bren barely contained his growl. Something had to be wrong with him. He never got jealous. He never even stuck around long enough to get jealous. So why was this female making him territorial? Is this what his brother had felt when he had met Jack? He did not like it. But, he disliked the clear connection between them even more. When he felt in control again, he looked at Rory, only to find her alone and studying him.

"If you think I didn't notice you glaring your way through the dining hall and nearly growling at people, you're all kinds of wrong. ¿Cuál es tu problema?" Then she murmured under her breath, "¡Joder! This is a bad idea. I should take him back."

"No!" Her eyes shot back up to his. They were glowing. Like staring directly into a blaze. He cleared his throat. "I am sorry for appearing to glare. I often look like I am scowling because of the scar." He lied. "I will attempt to look friendlier if you will allow me to stay and join you for the meal." He tried to give her a reassuring smile, but he had the feeling that she did not believe his explanation. "Food is one of my four favorite things."

"Ookaaay. Resting alien bitch face it is. Today's food options are in honor of Octoberfest. It's all German food and beer. Have you had any of that before?"

"No."

"Estás de suerte. We have some roast chicken and sausages over there. Next to that, we have some giant pretzels. Over here, we have potato dumplings and potato pancakes. We also have, käsespätzle which is a cheesy noodle and some sauerkraut. For dessert we have black forest cake and apple strudel. Then, there is all the beer. Just grab a tray, a plate, and anything you're interested in."

"It does sound like my lucky day." Bren could not believe the amount and variety of food they offered for just one meal. Humans were so very decadent, but since he was going to benefit from that fact he kept his opinion to himself. Instead, he grabbed two trays, multiple plates and piled on the food. Eating was something he was good at. He was a warrior and with his training, he ate a lot. He looked over at Rory's tray and his mouth dropped. She had two plates piled high with a third in her hand for the desserts. How could she possibly eat that much? "Are you feeding someone else? All that cannot be just for you."

He realized his mistake when he could feel her death stare. Then she turned away heading to one of the tables without another word. Once again, he followed. On the way, he noticed guards were stationed all around the room and he could only assume that they were there for him. He scoffed at the idea that they thought they could take him down.

That earned him another kill-you-with-her-eyes glare as she dropped off her tray and walked away to a nearby drink serving area. His tray landed with a loud clank as he quickened to do the same. He overheard her ordering something called a beer flight and so he did the same. It was a balancing act as he brought the row of three glasses each of different light to dark yellow liquids back to the table without spilling a drop. He sat down across from her and started eating.

Everything tasted so good, that he did not notice just how silent they were. Once he did, though, he could not take it any longer, so he said, "I did not mean to insult you. I just did not expect someone as small as you, to eat so much. I also grabbed a lot of food but I am a lot bigger and—"

"Oye, I have a very high metabolism. I require a lot of food or else I have no energy. It's fine." And then she just sat silent again.

Bren was inquisitive by nature so he continued to try to prod responses from her. For her part, Rory, frustratingly, ate on in silence.

Rory didn't know what to make of Bren. She was boiling mad at the aliens for kidnapping and keeping her bestie, but something about Bren was very disarming. He was clearly trying to get to know her and enjoying the food and well, he was just so fucking hot. Even the scar was turning her on. Okay. Especially the scar. She recalled all of Jack's descriptions of her intimacies with his brother while her mind and libido argued on the approach to take with him. Logic said he was the enemy. She needed to keep a close eye on him and keep her superior, distant, guard position in place. On the other hand, her libido tried to convince her head that getting close and intimate with all of his well-defined muscles would be both pleasurable and potentially a way to gather information. One thing she *was* sure of, she was done listening to him ramble. *¡Dios!*

"Have you tried the beer yet?"

He stopped talking and his eyes went a little wide in surprise. "You are speaking to me? I started to wonder if I was not really here."

Rory couldn't help the small laugh that escaped. As if his giant form could possibly be overlooked. Still, she couldn't let him off the hook that easily. "Maybe I just like to eat in silence?"

He looked around them. "You would be the only one. Everyone else is quite talkative."

"Are you saying I should be like everyone else?"

"No. Of course not. I am just pointing out that evidence shows most humans like to eat and talk at the same time. The Staraban do too. Some species do not, but I believe our species have this in common. I had to wonder, besides me being a prisoner, why we were not talking. I like to talk. Laugh. Discuss. And sometimes intimidate."

He gave her a goofy grin after the last one and sure enough, she couldn't help another little laugh. "I see. Now I know how to drive you crazy. Thank you for that information. I like to know my opponent's weaknesses. What else do I need to know about you?"

He stiffened with his beer half-way to his mouth. "Do we have to be opponents?"

"Claro. What would *you* call us?"

"I would call you many things. Opponent would not be one of them."

"I see." She paused and studied him, trying to make him squirm but he just stared right back at her waiting. "You never did answer me about the beer."

"I was just about to try the first one."

He lifted the glass and took his first sip of the first beer in the flight. His face transformed into a look of ecstasy and Rory couldn't help but wonder if that would be how he looked if they were to do a sampling of other things. Intimate things. She could smell her own arousal on the air and when she looked at him again, his eyes had turned a darker, more vibrant blue. She was convinced he could scent her too. *¡Mierda!*

She rushed to speak. "What did you think?"

"Think?" His eyes narrowed.

"Of the beer."

His face relaxed again. "It was interesting. The flavors played wonderfully along my tongue."

Before she even realized what she was doing or who she was doing it with, she flirted back, "And did your tongue enjoy playing?" *¡Ay, Dios mío! What did I just say?*

His voice came back deeper, all sensuality and silk sheets, "My tongue always enjoys playing."

Now her lust wasn't the only one permeating the air and his was downright intoxicating. *Get a grip, mujer. Shut it down.* "Well… That would be none of my business. Just keep your tongue to yourself, or I may have to remove it."

She finished her food and drank her beer as silence fell heavily between them. Again. *You have to watch yourself around this one.* Looking over, she saw that he was gulping down his beer—he had moved on to the second—and appeared to be studying her. She made sure she didn't squirm because, fuck that.

"What does your brother plan to do con mi amiga?"

"I do not know. They seem drawn to each other. I thought maybe your friend had done something to him. He has not been acting himself around her."

She cracked a smile at hearing that. "I thought the same thing about your brother and my friend, only it was him doing something to her. She hasn't been acting normally either. I'm worried, though, because she doesn't have a lot of experience with men. He better not hurt her."

"He does not hurt his partners."

"And you?"

"No. Not intentionally. Sometimes they get more attached than I expect and they are not pleased when I do what I say and leave after a night together."

She hadn't ever heard a guy be this forward about his playboy love 'em and leave 'em behavior. Okay. She could deal with that. She didn't exactly like sticky either. She was usually the one to leave in the middle of the night. Not because she was dishonest about a one-night stand, but because she also didn't want to give anyone a false impression by being there in the morning. "I can respect that. I have a similar approach to sexual encounters."

And suddenly he was growling at her. It seemed to surprise him as much as her. He looked at her sheepishly and said, "I am not sure why I did that. I apologize."

"Uh huh. Claro. Anyway. I see you are almost finished with your first flight of beer. Did you want more before you go back to your cell, um, room for the night?"

"I would enjoy more. Can I grab some more of the black forest cake and maybe some more sausages, as well?"

"You can have as much as you like."

Thirty minutes later, Rory couldn't decide if letting him get drunk had been a great idea or a really bad one. He was leaning on her and, damn, he was heavy. On the other hand, he was hella funny. She also couldn't help but feel a bit of a sadistic pleasure at knowing how badly he was going to feel the next morning. Yeah…if she couldn't hurt his brother for kidnapping her friend, at least she could watch Bren suffer.

She held off the other guards who tried to step in because she could handle a drunk Bren. She got him back to his room as he kept up a rambling commentary on Earth's foods, games he enjoyed playing, things he noticed as they passed, and especially a lot about his new favorite animal, los gatos. He went on and on about cats. Rory was laughing so hard, on the inside, as he described all the things he loved about cats. Their sleek fur, intelligent eyes, playful nature, evil nature, hunting skills, and how much he enjoyed curling up with his newly acquired pets to sleep and relax. It touched her a bit when he evinced concern over their well-being during his captivity. She hoped someone from his base would take care of the buggers.

They entered in darkness, but Rory had no problem seeing in the dark. As she tipped him into his bed, he murmured about how the room was spinning and how he hadn't known that humans had developed spinning rooms and how it was a great idea for torturing information out of someone. She didn't want to leave him completely clothed overnight, so she started tugging off his boots. She also decided he was right and it was time to get some information.

"Why did you really come to Earth?"

"It all in pamph-ph-ph-let."

She rolled her eyes even though he wouldn't be able to see it, "What is?"

"We learned about you—" he tweaked her nose with his finger, "—and we did not want let you die when you make peeee-tza and moovieees and other th… th… things."

"Who told you about us?"

"Sh-sh-shiny aliens."

"What?"

"Hmm."

She was losing him. Distracted with indecision about whether to strip him or leave him clothed, she didn't react quick enough when he reached up, grabbed her shoulder, and yanked. She fell across him and wound up face to face. Their eyes locked into each other and all she wanted to do was dive into the blue depths of his, swim a while, and luxuriate. She was so mesmerized that she hadn't noticed when exactly she had started rubbing her body up and down his like the cats he'd described before. More tenderly than she would have thought possible, with him being so far gone, he reached up and stroked her hair. Did he just pet her? He did it again. He was petting her! Probably like one of his cats. Lucky cats. Maybe, he even thought she *was* one of his cats. That made her snicker.

"So beautiful. So very…beautiful. Beau-ti-ful." He looked down at her lips and she forgot to have any thoughts at all. Her sex drive took the wheel, so she closed her eyes in anticipation of feeling his lips against hers. Nothing too deep. Nothing too intimate. She didn't want to do anything more without sober consent, but if he chose to press his lips to hers just for a second? He'd made it clear he wanted her. And despite her reflexive anger, she wanted him too. One, short, chaste kiss and then she would go. Before she changed her mind, she closed her eyes and waited for him to make his move. Waited. Waited. Tuning back into her other senses, she realized that his even breathing and slowed hearts rate, since the Staraban had two hearts, meant he'd fallen asleep. She opened her eyes and they confirmed her assessment. *Well, damn.*

A part of her acknowledged that she should be glad that nothing happened. Another part found it hard to feel gratitude while her lips still tingled with the near-pleasure, the almost-pleasure, the she-needed-to-find-her-battery-powered-friend pleasure. She gracefully rolled off of him, covered him with the blanket, locked him in, and found some new guards to post at his door.

She considered finding a non-battery-operated friend for the night, but something made her turn away from the idea. She enjoyed Bren's scent in her nose and all over her clothes. His face was on her mind and she didn't want someone else to alter any of it. She wasn't going to analyze that too deeply but she did have to wonder if this was what Jack had felt with her alien. Dear god, if it was, she was eventually going to be fucking that giant senseless, because if her awkward-around-guys friend couldn't resist, Rory didn't stand a chance. *¡Joder!*

[2]

THE PREVIOUS BATTLE

Captain's Log: Earth date October 9, 2025

Pues claro, we are on board the ship, but it wasn't because I made his stubborn ass see reason. My little secret makes it so easy to dupe everyone. They can't plan for what they don't know exists.

On top of that, I now have a secret weapon. My best friend Jack moved her Personal Assistant Link (PAL) to me. Hal is a fully functional AI that attaches subcutaneously, behind the ear. Jack taught Hal to hack into the alien computers using their common language called Standard Economic Language or SEL. Hal and I can also communicate silently with each other so no one is the wiser.

Makes me wonder if he and I could even stage a coup and take over the ship if we wanted... Hmm... I may have to consider whether or not to make it so.

Rory out.

CHAPTER 2

Staraban Base, Northern California

October 9, 2025

Rory led Jill through the base. She had scouted ahead and knew which ship Bren would be taking. It had been amazingly easy to get around unnoticed in her other form. She waved Jill over to crouch near her, behind a few of the crates waiting to be loaded onto said ship. She tapped at the back of her ear which was still a little sensitive and whispered, "Hal, you there?"

When Rory met with Jack and Jill to hatch a plan to stow her and Jill onto Bren's spaceship without his or Nial, his second-in-command's, knowledge, they concluded it made sense to send her with Hal. He would be great support and gave them a way to access and store data on the trip. He would be able to interface with the ship and help them stay under the radar. The only problem with Hal was that he had a sarcastic streak a mile long.

"Of course I'm here. Not that you care. You left me turned off for over twenty-four hours."

Rory hissed between her teeth, "Keep your voice down, dammit."

"Fine."

"Um. Great. Thanks. We're in the process of boarding."

"And by boarding you mean sneaking on."

"Uh, right. Claro que sí. We are aiming to board that giant clam with a tail and two horns looking ship. Could you please tell me if you are able to create a distraction by tapping into the Staraban system to draw them away from that ship?"

"What kind of distraction are you looking for?"

"Nothing too obvious or they may run a full diagnostic of the ship. Can you do subtle?"

"Of course I can do subtle. When I want. Hold on."

Rory looked back at Jill who returned her look with consternation. Jill was a new friend and Rory liked her quite a lot. She'd been given safe haven because she saved Jack and Tarc's lives before defecting from the cruel militia-group resistance movement called MAD, Make Aliens Dead, when they were captured. Jill had turned out to be the daughter of the militia leader, which was extra cringeworthy. Considering the prejudice Jill had been raised with, she'd been holding up pretty well in the face of working with the aliens and even more so with her friend Jack who was now an outed vampire in their group. "Jill. I know you're new to all this. Perhaps you want to reconsider coming?"

Jill shook her head. "Who the fuck do you think you're talking to? Do I look like a fucking fainting violet to you?" Subtle she was not.

"Bueno. Just wanted to give you an out if you wanted it. Try not to skewer me on the lance-sized darts your eyes are sending my way. I know you're new to the whole friends thing, but we're supposed to take care of each other and that was all I was trying to do. So, sheath your tongue and get ready to go at my signal."

Jill's shoulders, that had been up around her ears, slumped. "Fuck. Sorry. I'm ready when you are."

"Okay. Spikey." She could feel the point of Jill's eye-lance again as she took offense at the nickname given to her by Jack. If they were all going to be friends, Jill was going to have to get used to giving and taking jabs, because that's what friends were for.

"Okay. I've sent a message to all communication devices in this area asking them to check in with the main office but made it look like a glitch in the communication system. In one minute, you can make your way to the ship."

"Thanks, Hal. You're the best."

"Wow. Compliments. I'm already looking forward to being yours instead of Jack's."

Sure enough, Rory saw all the Staraban that had been working on loading containers onto the ship exit the area. She hissed. "Now."

She and Jill ran across and into the ship with their giant, overstuffed backpacks. Everything they could imagine needing for the next few months contained therein. Actually, they had no idea how long they would be in space, but they were willing to take the chance. Jill didn't have anyone who cared about her and in fact, the last intelligence they had gathered indicated that her father had issued a death sentence for her betrayal. Rory had Jack, Will, who was a mental hotbed of self-loathing since being turned into a vampire against his, well, will, plus a few casual friends on the base.

Other than that, she was a total free agent and this was something she wanted to do. Had to do. Of course, it had nothing to do with Bren. That thirst-trap alien could kiss her ass. She had tried to make him see reason. Had tried to get his permission to come. She'd tried and she'd failed.

Now, she could care less what he thought. She'd do what she always did, whatever the fuck she wanted. Clearly, Nial had failed to block Jill from coming as well. Both aliens were in for a smack-upside-the-head awakening for trying to tell Earth women what to do.

Earth girls may be easy, but they were also fierce as fuck. She would have thought Bren had learned his lesson the last time he'd tried to tell her what to do, but apparently he was still a dumbass.

Three days earlier…

"Why are you such a dumbass?"

Bren was not sure what exactly a dumbass was supposed to be but he could guess and it was not good. "You are being unreasonable." The look she sent his way was obviously dumbass take two. He did not know why his usual skill with a potential partner failed him so completely with this one. For the last two days, they had either been heating up for each other, or they were fighting each other. They did not seem to be able to talk in any other language.

His time as a prisoner had proven relatively comfortable with one exception, the fights with the only entity he seemed to want. There were other appealing humans at the HARM base and some had even made it clear they were interested in getting his attention. But no, his—maybe he should borrow her phrase—dumbass, seemed to only want this one very stubborn, very frustrating, very arousing, and totally infuriating female who refused to ever see reason. "How can you not see that playing with weapons is dangerous?"

Rory's expression was dumbass, round three. "I don't *play* with weapons. I work on and with weapons. I've done so for years and I don't see how it is any of your business. You are the prisoner, I am the guard, you need to just shut up, look pretty, and eat your damn food."

Bren could not hold back the growl that had been working its way up his throat throughout this disagreement. He stifled it with stuffing his mouth full of his overly delicious food. He now understood the difference between a hamburger and a gourmet hamburger. He also learned the difference between fries and truffle fries. Today's menu was all about elevated American food. Maybe the food would help him forget that Rory seemed intent on blowing her own head off. He did not have a full understanding of human weapons but the one she was taking apart and putting back together was definitely of the deadly variety. Just when he thought he could not get any more aggravated with her, she did something she purposefully knew would irritate him.

Bren had four things he loved: his family, sex, food, and his new favorite pets, Earth cats. And he was *not* into sharing two out of those four, though he was becoming less protective of the cats as he became more comfortable with them. The food, though? Absolutely not. And, she knew it from some of their earlier meals together, but in the middle of their current argument, she took a break from the weapon, reached over, and plucked up some of his truffle fries. She could go get her own, but no, she chose not to. Of course she chose not to. Instead, she chose to add fuel to their argument. *Infuriating female.*

He was about to tell her just what he thought of her guns and food stealing but his voice became trapped in his throat. Rory did what she had been doing to him since he arrived at HARM, she tied him up in knots of emotion. She took one of the confiscated fries and licked her way from one end to the other, keeping eye contact with him the whole time, and then stuck it in her mouth and pulled it out. She even threw in a moan. A *fashing* moan.

When she spoke, her voice came out deep and husky. "I just love licking up the truffle. It's so salty and flavorful. A girl enjoys a taste once in a while."

And just like that, all his irritation flamed into white hot lust. She did not fight fair. Nor did she ever seem to mean it. With a wink, she ate up the offending, lucky fry and went back to her previous dangerous activity. "You are cruel."

"Yes. I am. You should remember that. Don't tangle with me because I do bite." And his torturer snapped her teeth at him.

He flashed his own teeth. "So do I."

Heated silence descended upon them. At least until she reached over and grabbed more fries. They were still fighting over the fries when his brother, Tarc, showed up at the HARM base with Nial. His brother was looking for Jack, who had escaped. Maybe it was time for him to do the same. He had stayed mainly to keep the peace, but every day got harder. He wanted Rory too much and he did not like the feelings she generated within him. Jealousy. Longing. Obsession. It was especially galling considering she seemed to be so much less affected by their connection. And now... there was nothing to keep him there. Yes. It was time for him to gain some distance.

Turned out, Jack needed rescuing from another group of aliens, the Vrolan, who had originally commissioned the humans relocation, which was now in question. They quickly organized a rescue party made up of Tarc, Nial, Will, and Bren but, of course—he should have anticipated it—he and Rory got into another argument. Nothing new, and it was exhausting. She refused to stay behind. Why did she not understand how fragile she was? All humans were relatively easy to kill, but Rory, she was so small.

He could not even name the emotion he got every time he thought of her in danger, but as a result, anger coursed through him as she insisted on coming. On top of the danger of the rescue, he also did not like that Rory was offering to feed Jack her blood if it became necessary. It sat wrong with him thinking about watching Rory be hurt. Same as all the times before, he lost the battle with her and they all set out together. He was even more determined to keep a distance from her.

Present time…

"I cannot believe they did not even come to say goodbye," Nial said. Bren patted Nial on the shoulder. His friend sounded like Bren felt. They had just reached deep space, having left Earth's atmosphere thirty minutes before.

Their departure had been simple. They had walked Qisto, who had been responsible for their false commission as well as Jack's detainment and torture, onto the ship and placed him in a specially altered containment cell. They also created a unique suit to contain the Vrolan's deadly ability, namely shooting crystal shards out of his body. With Qisto well-contained in his suit and cell and all the supplies on board, they had all convened in the ship bay. Tarc and Jack were there as well as Caran, Tarc and Bren's sister. The fact that Will did not show was expected as the vampire was still struggling with his transformation. The fact that Rory and Jill had not come to say goodbye stung, and it was clear that he and Nial were both feeling that pain.

"I understand how you feel, but maybe it was for the best. After the argument with Rory in my room with the throwing knives, I was ready for a calm departure and I do not think that is what we would have had if those two had been there." Mostly true. He had wished to see her one more time. Her intense fire… no, he was not going to think on it now.

Nial gave a curt nod. "I think I will go check with engineering to see that all is as it should be, then check on our prisoner and make sure all is well there. I will see you at mid-meal."

"Good. I plan to start reading through all the information that Jack and Hal provided us and will see you then. And Nial?"

"Yes?"

"You could always try to find her when we get back."

"Who?"

Bren knew that Nial knew exactly who he meant, but clearly, the warrior and close family friend wanted to keep his feelings to himself. "No one. Just know that if you want to talk," he paused dramatically, "I am sure Caran would be happy to listen." They both chuckled. Talking may not be their strong suit, but they both knew the other was there if needed. That would have to be enough for now.

"Fuck off." With that, Nial wandered away. The warrior had clearly been spending too much time with Jill and her preference for the word fuck had transferred to him. Who was he kidding? That word had found its way into all of them. It was rather like the Drolta vine from New Staraba. Once it latches on, it is near impossible to dislodge.

Bren stared out the window of his office into the vastness of space and wished he did not feel quite so much connection to the emptiness around them.

"I can't believe we did it. We are in fucking space." Jill just shook her head, face full of disbelief.

"I know. So damn exciting. I just wish I could look out a window or something. I'm sure it's beautiful." Rory was a ball of delighted, nervous energy. She wanted to go explore and she needed to get them food soon. They had been in space for a few Earth hours and hunger was setting in. She required some serious sustenance. "I'm going to go sneak into the area with food with Hal's help. I need you to stay here and out of sight, deal?"

"I could come with you, you know. I'm not helpless. In fact, I'm fucking capable as fuck."

Rory stopped her there, "I know you're not helpless and very capable—"

"I bring that up a lot, don't I."

"I'm afraid so, chica. I was starting to wonder about it, but didn't want to pry. ¿Sabes?"

"As the leader's daughter, I could never be good enough, strong enough, cruel enough. I guess I'm used to having to defend myself. The easiest way to do it was to be a bitch every time someone dared to question my capabilities."

Rory grabbed her friend's hand. "I have no doubt in my mind that you are fucking fierce. But I can talk to Hal in my head, silently, and react to his instructions. If I have to convey that information to you, it makes the chance of us getting caught go up. ¿Vale?"

Jill seemed to think it over, probably looking for holes in the logic. Rory understood. She wouldn't want to be left behind either. Jill finally nodded. "Yeah. You're right. I'll wait, but I'm not happy about it."

"Understood. I'll be back soon." The truth was that while all she'd told Jill was technically accurate, the real reason Rory wanted to go solo was that she was planning to use her hidden skills to prowl the ship and she wasn't quite ready to share that knowledge with Jill. She planned to make sure that, by the time Bren or Nial learned of their unwanted guests, they would be too far into the trip to be returned back to Earth.

Rory silently made her way out of the room they had chosen to hide in. It was a supply room filled with lots of crate-like devices. The crates swirled with some form of protective energy. They learned early on not to touch them unless they wanted to get zapped with an electric-like shock. From Hal, who had hacked into the ship system, they learned that this supply room was filled with things needed for a later part of the trip, which theoretically meant, no one should be in there for some time. As soon as Rory entered the hall, she touched behind her ear and thought, "Hey Hal, I need you silent mode."

Hal thought back at her, "Sure, Rory. Need another distraction?"

"No. I need you to direct me to the food area avoiding all the Staraban. I believe they should be done with lunch by now. Can you make sure I am right and find me a path to it?"

"Sure. No probs."

"No probs? Who have you been hanging with?"

"Can't an advanced being choose to learn some slang?"

"Advanced being?" She thought that at him with her most sarcastic mental voice.

"You know what I mean. Now. Are you planning on doing this food hunt in human form or cat form?"

Rory's adrenaline and energy were high just as they always were before she shifted. "I plan to be in cat form. I'll be so much more stealthy in that form."

"Agreed. Will you need some litter though?"

"Har har. Are you going to throw cat jokes at me the whole trip?"

"Pretty much."

"Okay. At least I'm forewarned so I can just ignore you. Is that how Jack usually dealt with you?

"Pretty much."

"Good to know. Shifting now, but I should be able to communicate with you mentally."

"Before you do, you will want to head into the room across the way. There is a venting system with an entry point that connects with the one that will take you to their version of a mess hall."

"I would high five you for this if I could. Gracias." Hal mumbled to himself something about bodies being overrated, but of course, his mind and hers were linked, so, she'd heard him anyway.

Now she just needed to evade the two knuckleheads-in-charge and their overly muscled minions over the next few days. As a panther shifter, she was used to being the hunter, but there was still a thrill running through her at hiding out in the shadows in evasion. This cat and mouse game was going to be fun, even if she was playing at being the mouse. Bren would eventually learn to stop underestimating her because she was no mouse, she was the whole fucking cat-in-caboodle.

She quietly made her way into the room and pulled out her handy-dandy Swiss Army knife. After attempting a few different tools, she found a way to pull off the vent cover and was ready to go prowling.

Hal thought at her, "Good work."

"Thanks. Shifting now."

Unlike some of the shifter romances she had read in the past, there was nothing painful in her people's shifting. It wasn't that her body had to undergo a physical change, the shifting power was based in magic. Her panther was always with her. They just existed in different dimensions, in a way. Shift and her human form disappeared into the alternate space and the panther was present. Shift again, and her panther was displaced with her human form at the ready. Both were always there, always her, and always connected.

Not that there were no body alterations. There were a few. Her people could take on simple aspects of their alternate selves. Just like the panther retained her human higher thinking, her human form could elongate her nails into claws or canine teeth into fangs. It's magic, so no one questioned when certain aspects of the one appeared on the other. For a full body swap, though, she just needed to close her eyes and ta-dah, species swap.

Her panther form was bigger than a normal panther. Every time she tried to picture having to actually transition the way books or movies described it, from one body to the other, she cringed at the image. *Fuck, no.* She wasn't sure if she would *ever* want to shift in that scenario.

Thankfully, not a problem and so she shifted. As her panther swapped dimensions with her human form, she stretched her front paws forward and arched her back. The stretch felt amazing. She looked up into the vent and with one graceful leap, silently landed inside.

"Nice." Hal sounded properly impressed.

She thought back, "Thanks. Which way from here?"

It took a few minutes with some stops and starts, but Hal did his thing and led her to the right room. She needed to wait a few minutes for a couple of stragglers to exit, but soon all was silent below. Shifting again, Rory pulled out her tool and with some maneuvering, was able to pop the cover open. "I hope I'll be able to pop it back in."

"We'll figure something out."

"Are we still good below?"

"Yep. And there are no Staraban in the vicinity."

Thinking no more, she jumped down into the shared eating room and looked around. "Okay. Now where do they keep their food?"

"See the machine to the side that looks like an ATM?"

"Yes."

"Just go up to it and request what you need. Lucky for you, they have programmed in some Earth foods."

"That is lucky. I admit I hadn't thought of this scenario. Bad on me."

Rory walked up and with Hal's direction, was able to order up a feast of food in packages, water, and some snacks. She placed it all into the backpack she had brought with her. "This was almost too easy. There's no fun in that."

"So you're one of them."

"One of them?"

"Adrenaline junky." She could swear she heard him sigh in her head. "Why me? What did I do to deserve this?"

"What are you talking about?"

"You do realize that my existence is now tied to yours, right? So I want you to be a safety junky not a thrill seeker."

She chuckled softly. "I'm afraid that ship has sailed my friend."

"Fucking fantastic."

"Don't worry, Hal. We are going to have quite the adventure together."

"That's what I'm worried about."

She chuckled some more at his thoughts as she considered how to attach the covering again. She pulled out a tiny hook and some rope from a pocket in her backpack and attached the grate to the hook. "This should do the trick." Using one of the tables and her natural agility, she jumped up into the vent, yanked the covering into place and tied the rope to one of the hand holds within the vent. She shifted back to her panther form for stealth, and made her way back to the room she started in.

Once there, Hal told her when she could cross over to the storage room. She shifted back to her human form before entering so as to keep Jill in the dark. She felt a bit guilty about it, but trusting wasn't something she did lightly. The friendship was still new and while Jill seemed to have taken the news that Jack was a vampire in stride, Rory figured there was still plenty of time for show-n-tell. No need to test the limit of Jill's ability to accept yet another new unbelievable thing. They were about to spend a lot of time together.

[3]

HIDE AND CAT

Captain's Log: Earth date October 12, 2025

It's been an interesting trip through space so far. I'm keeping my secret hidden from Jill, which isn't easy. But, I'm just not ready to share all of me, despite growing closer to her. Despite the guilt. Despite how much more difícil it gets as she has started coming on many of our outings. In fact, that first day, we located some of the unused quarters and make regular trips there to get clean and take care of business.

When she doesn't come, Hal and I have had a great time skulking through the ship. We tell Jill it's reconnaissance and it is that too. But, we are mostly messing with the warriors wandering around. I give them a good chase and he erases all the evidence leaving everyone confused. I get bored easily, what can I say.

Honestly, though, it's been almost too easy. It's as though the crew can't be bothered with proper security while on board the ship. Have they never had stowaways before? Maybe not. All the better for us. Space is... not as exciting as you might think. It's kind of empty. Most of the time when we look out of the windows we run across, it's just dark out. The blanket of faraway stars is beautiful, but that's all it is. Even with my special sight, I can only catch colors and lights, but nothing truly spectacular. I guess it won't get really interesting until we get nearer to somewhere.

Speaking of getting near, I think that Jill has her suspicions. Luckily, she isn't asking. I just need more time. Other thoughts, I'm having? I wonder if I'm the first shifter in space. Not according to the romance books I've read, but that's all just fiction. Of course, so are shifters.

Rory out.

CHAPTER 3

Staraban Ship, Space

October 12, 2025 Earth Date

Bren slammed his palm into the table. On the inside he reconsidered his ill-advised display of frustration. Big, strong leader that he was, he tried not showing that his hand was aching. But, Nial called him on it.

"Hurts. Huh?"

"So much. *Shet!* And still is not as angering as these reports. How is it that a giant black cat, not one of mine by the description, is aboard my ship and yet none of our cameras are picking anything up? How is it possible?"

Nial looked like he might want to plow his hand into the table as well. "I cannot explain it. Unless our warriors are all experiencing the same delusion, which makes even less sense, then we somehow have a big cat on board and it is also somehow affecting the cameras. It would be easier if it was one of yours."

"As though I would be so careless as to let my pets roam the ship's hallways." He scoffed. His furballs, as he learned on Earth to call them, were well taken care of in the captain's quarters. They had no need to go exploring. "Do we have any information about the Vrolan that would hint at something like this? Perhaps our prisoner Qisto has more tricks we do not know about?" A few days back, when Qisto had shot a shard into Jack, nearly killing her, they had not known he was capable of that skill. Perhaps Vrolans at the Ambassador level had other skills that no one knew about? Bren thought that sounded logical, but a cat? And how was he able to manipulate the cameras while he was still locked up? He shook his head as he negated his own questions.

"I see you are reaching the same conclusion that I have, which is that I cannot see a way for Qisto to be doing what is described."

"Then what? I need answers. I will not bring a ship carrying an unknown, potentially dangerous situation to the AAA headquarters."

"I agree. We must find a way to capture this cat. I recommend a search of the ship from top to bottom starting with the least populated areas as they are more likely to be a hiding space."

"I agree."

A few hours later, Bren felt even more frustrated. They had not located the cat, but that was not the most angering thing about their current situation. That honor was given to the fact that they *had* located Rory and Jill on board hiding out and now he was downright murderous.

"What the fuck were you thinking?" he bellowed.

Rory just glared back. Did the female have no fear at all? Not that he would ever really hurt her but he knew he presented an intimidating figure just by scowling and he was sure his face was far past that.

He growled at her. "I am waiting for your answer."

"You already know the answer so it's a stupid question and I don't feel the need to answer stupid questions." She shrugged. She actually shrugged.

Bren growled again. "How have you evaded detection this whole time? Eaten? Taken care of other needs? Or do you find all questions stupid?"

She shrugged again, the maddening female. "No. They aren't all stupid."

He waited for her to deign to answer the non-stupid questions but that was all she said. Nothing else. Nothing at all that might convince him that throttling her was not a good idea. He looked over at Nial, in the hope the warrior might help him regain his ability to reason, but he and Jill were glaring at each other just as hard. What a *fashing* mess. Just then Rory sighed and he hoped it meant she was going to give him something, anything to work with. His hope was premature.

"What's done is done, hombre. It's too late to return us to Earth, so let's focus on the future, shall we?"

"What future is that exactly?" He glowered.

"The one where we are included on your mission to talk to triple A." She snickered.

He could not believe she snickered. He still did not understand what was funny about that name. "I do not see anything funny about this."

"That's because you're a stick in the mud."

He was not sure what exactly a stick in the mud meant but considering the tone she used, she clearly had just insulted him. He was having none of this situation. "I think I will stick you both in a cell for the duration of this trip." Her horrified look went a long way to finally mollify his anger. She never liked it when he had the upper hand and on his ship, he always had the upper hand. She was going to learn that well enough.

He was doing great until she began walking, no, prowling up to him. Her hips, he really liked her hips, were swinging as she made her way closer. No. He would not be swayed by her hips. "You want to tell me that you didn't miss me at all?"

"What?" He dragged his gaze from the most perfect hips in any galaxy and looked into her eyes as he tried to make sense of what she had said. Unfortunately, he continued in a fog because of her gorgeous sensual eyes that often had a teasing edge to them, like they did now.

"I keep telling you we make a better team than adversaries. Let me prove it to you."

No. She was not going to get the upper hand. He was going to stand firm and that was how it would be.

"I don't know how you did it, but way to fucking go." Jill was sitting in a seemingly relaxed pose on one of the beds in their new quarters munching a bar of chocolate. After rooming together for days, though, Rory knew the position for what it was. If anything came through their door, uninvited, Jill would spring into action in the blink of an eye.

"It's nothing." Rory turned back to the ATM, grabbed the plate of brazo de gitano, and walked over to sit on her own serviceable, though far from comfortable, bed. They were a far cry from luxury accommodations, but a major upgrade from living in a storage room. They could make this work just fine. At least it came with its own nanobot washing room thing. Other than that, a small platform hung off one wall with a couple of chairs around it. She had spent enough time on the Staraban base to know that often the walls hid closets and other useful structures. They would have to explore later.

"I do find it interesting, Jill, that we both grew up in a world where we lost our mothers and found ourselves at the mercy of the men around us. You learned to defend yourself one way and I learned a different way. I learned to get the upper hand by being fully in control of my sexuality and be the deadliest person in the room."

"And I learned to hide all sexuality and stick to killing or hurting anyone who got near me, which also meant being the deadliest person in the room."

"Exactly. Two sides of the same coin. The basic outcome being, we live at the whim of no man." She grinned.

"Amen to that." Jill grinned back.

"Have I mentioned how glad I am that you decided to defect when you did, Spikey?" She hadn't been there when it happened, but the story Jack and Jill told about it sounded both harrowing and amusing. Also, Rory knew just how much the other woman enjoyed Jack's nickname for her.

"I would throw something at you, but all I have at-hand is my chocolate and that's staying right here. What are you eating?"

"It's a dessert from the region in Spain where I grew up. It is called brazo de gitano and it's a rolled sponge cake with the filling of your choice. I may have had Hal program the machines to make it for me."

"What filling did you give it?"

"I went with mermelada de naranja or orange marmalade. The oranges remind me of home too and I didn't want anything too sweet."

"Sounds delicious."

"One of my favorites." Memories from her childhood rushed in. Her mamá and her bringing in fresh oranges to make the marmalade that would eventually go into her famous mermelada de naranja. The quiet evenings spent hunting through the woods for dinner followed by Papá always joking that he needed to take a second helping of cake to taste if it was the best one mama had ever made. Singing together into the night. Those were some of her favorite memories. She tuned back in to hear Jill ask her a question in a tone that said this wasn't the first time she asked it.

"Could you tell me more about where you come from? I know you mentioned Spain."

"Southern Spain actually, Andalusia. The people are as warm as the summer sun. There are problems like everywhere else, but there is something magical about the music, the food, the dancing… the overall atmosphere. Very different than these cold, bland metal walls." She waved her hand to indicate their room.

"Sounds like you miss it a lot. When was the last time you went for a visit?"

She tensed as she realized just how much of her history she was sharing with Jill. It felt somehow both uncomfortable and also a relief. It was so rare that she let anyone in beyond the walls she'd built, that every time she did, there was a moment of discomfort to deal with first. She took a deep breath and leaned just a little more in the direction of trusting her. "I haven't been back since I was a teenager. Let's just say I left under difficult circumstances I'm not yet ready to talk about, and I won't be going back."

"I understand. It will take me some time to unpack and share everything that I lived through growing up in a militia."

That gave Rory pause as her own story was tragic, for sure, but like her recent trip down memory lane can attest, at least she was loved by her parents and had those wonderful days as a family before it all went to shit. What must Jill's upbringing have been like? She could only speculate at how bad it was. A shudder, she tried to hide, ran through her. Looking the other woman directly in the eyes, she said, "I'm here if you want to talk. ¿Vale?"

"Yes. I'll let you know. So… how about another topic?"

Her friend was valiantly suppressing her own matching shudder. Then her lip curled into a sly grin. The look in her eyes told Rory she probably wouldn't like what was coming next, so she stuffed her mouth full of the delicious cake and indicated with her hand for Jill to continue.

"Do you really want to tell me that nothing has happened between you and Bren? I mean, the tension between you could have been cut by one of your knives."

Rory laughed. "That is highly amusing coming from you."

"What do you mean?"

"You and Nial?"

"That asshole?"

"The lady doth protest too much, me thinks, and blusters too strong in his presence." Rory arched a questioning eyebrow.

"I hate you. How dare you quote the bard at me?"

"He does seem to have a line for almost anything."

"Okay. That topic is now closed and we're moving onto a safer topic. Now what?"

"Now, amiga, we enjoy the rest of the trip and see if we can make ourselves useful."

"You think they will allow us to be useful?"

"¿Permitir? No one," Rory made air quotes, "'allows' me anything. Didn't we just say we don't live at their whims?"

"True. I'm in. At least after I try some of your cake."

"Bitch, get your own." She used the most dramatic offended tone she could.

Jill just glared, "And here I thought friends shared."

"I'd be more likely to share a kidney than to share my dessert."

Jill's response was to flash her middle finger on her way to the food ATM where she ordered her own dessert as God and all that is holy decrees it.

With that settled, Rory outlined a plan. "I think I'll visit the control, engine, and munitions rooms. My engineering skills should come in handy somewhere."

"I think I'll visit the munitions room with you. Good to acquaint myself with the weapons I might want to use if I somehow misplace all of mine."

"Let's hit that first then." They both nodded and stuffed more cake into their mouths allowing a moment of silence to appropriately and deeply appreciate their dessert.

"Bren and Nial are going to flip their fucking lids." Jill's smile was full of mischief and Rory couldn't remember the woman smiling much at all before.

"That will just make the visit that much sweeter." She couldn't help herself. Making Bren lose his shit was becoming her favorite pastime. That probably made her not a very nice person, but she never claimed otherwise. She winked at Jill and chewed on her final bite of cake.

"You want to explain to me what just happened?" Nial asked pacing in front of Bren's desk.

As he flopped into his desk chair he wished he had an answer, but the last twenty minutes were all a bit of a blur. He distinctly recalled what his plans *had* been, but somewhere between her approaching him and now, instead of a cell, the females had one of the bigger available quarters that had a personal Food Delivery Assistant, known as an FDA, and private hygiene facility. It might have something to do with what Rory had whispered in his ear. It might have something to do with his generally protective nature. It might even have something to do with how long he had gone without sex. Whatever had happened, he needed to put a stop to it. He was the one in charge of the mission, and they would not be safe if he could not stay in control. "*Fash.* I do not know, but it does not matter. It happened and despite what we both wish was true, it would not make sense to return them to Earth now. We must proceed with them on board."

Nial growled and looked about to pick up one of Bren's new cat figurines decorating his desk like he might throw it so he swiftly grabbed it out of reach. "No! You desecrated my meeting room figures on Earth, you may not hurt these. Get control of yourself."

"I am. Okay. I will. I just hate having Jill here. She might be deadly by Earth standards but we both know that is not the same as what we could encounter out here. She is too sure of herself and it could get her hurt or killed."

"You think Rory is not the same? She is and I share your concerns, friend. We will have to be vigilant and make sure to control the situation as best we can."

"Yes. Controlling the situation has proven easy to do up until now." Nial replied sarcastically.

He had no way to respond to that. After a few beats of his dual-hearts, he finally queried, "How long do you think we have before they get into trouble?"

"I will assume they already are. Ten minutes have passed since we left them."

"Computer. Locate humans Rory and Jill."

A voice came from the intercom in his office and said, "They are in the corridor outside the munitions room." He jumped up knocking his seat to the ground and was out the door, Nial right behind him, even before the voice stopped speaking.

A minute later —if that long— they came to an abrupt halt in front of the two confused looking guards assigned to protect the armory.

"What's happened? Where are the human females?"

The guards' faces contorted with concern, or maybe guilt, but one answered. "They said that you made them a part of the crew. The smaller one said that she was an expert at making weapons and would need to evaluate what we had to be able to do her job."

"And you did not think to contact me to verify the story?" He had not realized he had violent tendencies until that female entered his life. Warriors were meant to be protectors who turned to violence as a last resort and yet he was aching to punch these warriors.

They clearly saw they had made a mistake because the other stammered, "We were going to do that, but they were very convincing. At least, at the time. You arrived just after they went in and we were discussing how they had gotten past us without contacting you. We are not sure exactly why we let them in."

He grumbled under his breath, "That seems to be going around." He realized he could not be too angry when they—well, she—had the same effect on him. "Next time you have a dubious interaction with them, contact me before they even open their mouths."

His warriors stood with more confidence again, "We shall."

He looked over at Nial and they both took a fortifying breath before stepping into the room.

He stopped breathing as he took in the scene before him. Jill was lifting a multi-shot laser gun as though testing its weight. Rory was at a center table with a partially, dismantled disruptor. His lungs burned as he took in air again.

Stay calm. Stay in control. Deep breaths. Stay calm.

"What the fuck do you think you are doing? You have been in here for just a few minutes! How have you already destroyed one of our disruptors?"

"Is that what this is? How does it work?"

Stay fashing calm.

"Do you want to tell me why you destroyed something when you did not even know what it was?"

She shrugged. He was growing to hate that shrug. What was he thinking? He was not growing to hate it. He definitely hated it. She continued, "I don't need to know what something is called to learn the inner workings."

"The inner workings?"

"Yes. You seem to be unable to keep this information in your head, but I. Am. A. Munitions. *Expert.*" She slowly emphasized each word.

It felt like the giant *rapan* claw cutting into him all over again, only unlike the scar on his face, the attack was to his insides. Though imagined, it was equally painful. She did not respect him at all. *At all.* He replied coldly, "There is more to that sentence *you* seem to forget. Munitions expert *on Earth*. You are not *on Earth* nor dealing with human technolo—"

"I'm not stupid as you seem to think. I was very careful to inspect every piece and connection and—"

"You are not hearing me, Rory. Whatever else happens, listen to what I am saying to you right now. What you just dismantled, with no training or knowledge, could have disrupted this whole section of the ship if you had triggered the self-destruct function. Not only could these weapons hurt you very badly or kill you, but they could take this whole ship and all of its crew with you. All because your assumptions are based on inferior human technology." He paused to catch his breath. Just the thought of what could have happened… He wanted to shake some sense, respect for his authority, self-preservation, anything, something into her. He clenched his hands at his sides instead. "I am responsible for every single person on this ship and you may have avoided being put in a cell before, but if I cannot trust you to not kill everyone on board, you will force me to act for the safety of everyone. Before you answer me, as your Earth phrase about cats states, sheath your claws and consider your words."

She started to snicker at his last statement, but then met his gaze and sobered. *Good. Maybe she realizes how serious I am.*

"Bueno. I concede your point. I'll be more careful in the future and will endeavor to learn about everything before touching it. But. I *will* learn about your weapons. With help or without. This is what I am trained for and if you are truly concerned for my safety, you will allow it. The more I know, the better I can defend myself. ¿Entendido?"

He grudgingly had to agree. She too, had made her point. Both females would potentially need to know how to use the weapons. "Agreed. I will get someone to train you and Jill on the use of our weapons."

"*What?*" The angry outburst came from Nial.

"You heard me. Rory is correct. If we want them to be safe, the best thing we can do for our bloodthirsty Xena warrior women is to teach them how to properly defend themselves."

"What do you know of Xena?" Jill asked with an arrogantly raised eyebrow.

"We watched many of your entertainments as we learned about the species we were planning to help relocate."

"So who did you think Xena should be with?" Rory interrogated.

"Gabrielle." He answered quickly.

A huge smile spread across Rory's face, "Right answer."

Jill said, "I can't believe the alien Hercules knows as much about nineties pop references as we do. Honestly, I'm still half convinced I'm getting punked."

"Punked?" Nial asked.

"Oh look! There's something left they haven't seen." This from Rory.

"But we can find out." He headed toward the entrance.

"Great. You should totally go look that up."

"And take Nial with you. I'd hate for him to be left in the dark," Jill said.

The females had him and Nial at the door and somehow about to leave when he realized what they had almost accomplished. He paused to the side and ushered Jill and Nial through the door first. Rory's heat and scent were directly behind him as he waved his hand and closed the door, spun around, and pinned her against it. "Nice try. gatita."

"What did you call me?"

"Kitten. I believe it is a human term of endearment. No? And the language you seem to prefer at times is Spanish. Correct?"

"Well, yes to both. But there is no need for an endearment between us." She sounded nervous, maybe for the first time he could recall.

Bren leaned in, bending his knees to match her height, and rubbed his nose up her neck, feeling the shiver that ran through her body. Her breathing quickened and his dual hearts started to race in response. He whispered into her ear. "Are you sure about that, gatita?"

Her voice grew huskier as she said, "No." Her hands moved up his arms and every spot they touched was set aflame, even through his uniform.

He leaned in even closer. So close, he could almost feel the press of her breasts against his chest. Her pelvis against his groin. Almost. He hovered a bare breath of space away and inhaled the scent of their blended arousal in the air. His cock grew hard and heavy with lust. He wanted to taste her. To taste all of her. They had been teasing each other—well, she had been teasing him—for a while now and he was ready—beyond ready—for more. He drew her earlobe into his mouth and sucked, biting down gently with his teeth.

Her breath hitched, then she groaned and it went straight to his even harder cock. He released her earlobe and rubbed his nose along her cheek until they were face to face, their breaths mingling. It was the first time he had felt in control of their sensual foreplay and he liked it. A lot. He looked down into her proud face. Her eyes closed and her skin, so warm and so soft, was lightly flushed.

He licked her full bottom lip with the tip of his tongue and got his desired response. She gasped and he dove in. His mouth slanted over hers as his tongue plunged deep, tasting her. Her hands gripped his shoulders almost painfully, her nails feeling like sharp claws. She kissed him back with abandon. For once, utterly in the moment with him. *My Goddess, she tasted magnificent.* He had expected sweetness, though he should have known better, what he got was infinitely more enticing. She was spices and passion. The deeper the kiss went, the more complex her taste.

This female enflamed him more with one kiss than most of his partners could with sex. It took a while for his wits to come back to him, but he felt when she tensed and began to withdraw. That was when he heard the knocking. Apparently, Nial and Jill were wondering what was happening with them. He lifted his head, his lips hovering just above hers. He watched as her eyes fluttered open and he thought he might just fall right into them. Into the depths of golden-hazel pools nearly eclipsed by the passion-dilated black of her pupils.

Her clutching hands released him and he felt the detachment like a severing of something vital. He almost yelled out "no" and just barely contained the word within. He stepped back and pulled her away from the door. That was his mistake.

Jill had apparently been trying to get through the door to the point of attempting to hit it, because once the sensors sensed that no one was leaning on it, the door slid open and Jill ran through smacking into both of them and hurtling them to the ground. Nial, who tried to stop her, became imbalanced and landed on top of everyone else.

He heard his friend grunt in pain and had to assume that Jill had done something to him because next she yelled, "Get off me you big oaf!"

Rory, who was prone next to him, was laughing hysterically, which he had to assume meant she was unharmed, and since that was all he really cared about, he just lay there staring at the ceiling wondering where he had gone wrong in his life.

[4]

THE NAKED NEEDS

Captain's Log: Earth date October 16, 2025

Getting caught turned out to be the best thing that ever happened to us. The room they gave Jill and me couldn't be any better, and being able to spend my time learning alien tech instead of just figuring out how to survive in hiding is a million times more exciting. Sí, it would be even better if I could test some of the changes I would like to implement, but that was not meant to be at this time. The real negative spot on it all, is that my body can't forget the kiss we shared no matter how hard I try to convince it to do so. I've had many lovers and never felt like *that*. I thought it meant a turn in our relationship, but his body must not have felt the same. I even considered briefly taking one of these other alien hotties to my bed for some sport, but I couldn't work up even an ounce of the excitement Bren stirs just by walking into the room. Bastard. Who gave him the right to leave me like this? ¡Joder!

Anyway, considering all of their warnings about the dangers to be found in space, it has been completely blah. Just an unending voyage into the uneventful unknown. I think I'll go get some physical exercise to use up some of this excess, ehem, hunger I'm trying to forget about. Again.

49

Rory out.

CHAPTER 4

Staraban Ship, Space

October 16, 2025 Earth Date

"¡Oye! Shakar. I can't believe this thing actually runs. Are you sure we're in space?" Rory teased the flustered Staraban engineer from where she sat in the engine room looking over the newly translated schematics of the ship on the screen in front of her. Shakar glared back and grumbled something under her breath. Rory laughed. She probably deserved whatever she'd mumbled.

"When I was still in Jack, I admit, I hadn't realized what a mean streak you possessed. I'm actually impressed." This from Hal in her head.

"That's quite a compliment from you." She thought back.

"I know. I've been studying the schematics as well and I have to agree with you. Their technology is clearly ahead of us, but it's also messy as hell."

"It really is."

She still couldn't quite believe she'd convinced Bren to let her study the ship's design. What could have possessed him, she wasn't sure. Considering where they started, his prohibiting her from coming along, this was a pretty huge step.

It was also necessary and, therefore, appreciated. It had only taken her a couple of days studying similar manuals in munitions to understand all of the different types of weapons available. She had been excited to draw up modifications that she wanted to begin working on, but that died a sad death when Bren reminded her about the dangers of explosions and mishaps in space. Whatever.

Of course, that left her bored and when she approached Bren about allowing her to study the ship and especially the engine, she was ready for the fight she expected to happen. What she hadn't been prepared for was his easy acquiescence. When he agreed, she literally felt her jaw drop. Luckily, he had been distracted at the time, so he hadn't seen it and by the time he looked up at her from his desk, she had recovered. At least outwardly. Internally, she had to acknowledge that while she should have felt elated or at the very least relieved, she instead felt disappointed.

Ever since their interlude in the weapons room had been interrupted, Bren had been distant. Accommodating Jill and Rory's needs, sure, but uninvolved. A part of her had been looking forward to fighting with him because at least that would mean some form of engagement.

Rory shook off her wandering, uncomfortable thoughts and continued her study of the ship. The alien technology, as much as she liked to harass the easily annoyed Shakar, might be a tragic example of disorganization, but it was also fascinating. So many things for her brain to happily absorb. The one thing Rory couldn't stand was when her brain had nothing to work on, so she had made studying her way to pass the time.

When she wasn't doing that, she was joining Jill for weapons and fight training. As though Jill hadn't been deadly enough before, she was getting to be quite proficient at all the new weapons and fighting techniques. Nial and a few other warriors worked with them both and praised their advances. Well, Nial didn't. But, whatever. Nothing seemed to please the surly alien. He and Jill were still regularly at each other's throats, and Rory hated to admit that she was actually a little jealous of them.

Rory refocused on the schematics, trying to shake off her wandering thoughts. Trying to concentrate. Trying and failing. A few minutes later she admitted defeat. Apparently, she was done for the day. Maybe she needed to go hit something. Preferably a tall Staraban commander who was pissing her off. She sighed and then smiled. The easiest way to avoid admitting she missed the big lug was to get back to some good old mischief.

That thought finally cheered her up.

"You ready to go have some fun, Hal?" She questioned mentally.

"Always." He agreed enthusiastically.

Bren was already having a bad day and it had just gotten worse. He had been working hard to unravel the Vrolan's plot based on the information Jack and Hal had gotten from the Vrolan base on Earth, but the encryptions, misdirection, and the depth of the deception all kept him busy every minute he was not dealing with the basic day-to-day running of his crew and ship, not to mention dealing with their prisoner and unsuccessful attempts at interrogation. He did not really have a choice. When they arrived at AAA, he would go before the Assembly and have to present all of the data. He had to make sure the information was organized and easy to describe in a simple straight-forward manner. So far, with there being so many things they did not know, he was not sure the Assembly would even believe them or take their allegations seriously.

He could not let his brother, ARC, Earth and all of its inhabitants, nor Rory down. His gut was all twisted up for so many reasons.

A part of him was happy for the distractions that kept him away from the female who invaded his every unguarded thought but another part of him, his cock, was quite frustrated by the lack of contact between them since that passionate kiss against the door. He ignored that part by diligently and legitimately staying busy. That… and pleasuring himself three times a day, because she was as invasive as the Earth plants known as weeds.

It was still hard to believe that he had let her begin studying his ship without a fight. When she had walked into his office, she had been wearing a tight black tank top and leggings that hugged every delicious curve. He purposefully had not looked directly at her because if he had, well, he would not have kept his distance. Unfortunately, he responded too quickly to her questions in an attempt to get her to leave as fast as possible. He should have paid closer attention. Of course, if he had who knew where they would be now.

Probably one of them would be dead. They seemed combustible together.

He was not usually the one who played it safe, but he could not risk the overall morale of his crew. Morale that was now being threatened again with a new sighting of the damn giant black cat that no one could actually catch, not even on camera. The sightings had died down for a while but now he was getting reports from all over his fucking ship. *Fash!*

As he read the latest and most detailed report, he was thrown back to the day they fought with the Vrolan on Earth.

The rescue was underway and Bren saw the most beautiful thing he had ever seen, besides Rory. Will, at the time still fully human, was busy battling one of the Vrolan guards. The diamond-like aliens being extremely hard to kill, and it was clear, even with his special military background, he was struggling. Humans are easy to hurt and weaker than most of the aliens in the Alliance. He and Tarc were about to head over to help, when a giant black cat joined the fight tearing into the Vrolan's unprotected eyes. It was magnificent.

The strangest thing was that, when the Vrolan was dead, the giant cat jumped away and ran into the woods instead of attacking anyone else. As though it just showed up in time to help them. He had researched big cat behaviors and nothing had accounted for that. It seemed a very strange coincidence that the descriptions his warriors gave seemed to match the other big cat.

Great. Now he was coming up with cat conspiracy theories. He needed a break.

"Computer. Where is Nial at this moment?"

The ship's computer responded with, "In the training room."

That actually sounded like the perfect break. Maybe the two of them could spar some of his frustration out. He got up and swiftly made his way down the various corridors, first to his room to change out of the tan uniform the Staraban wore while working into the relaxed pants used during training. Dressed, he jogged to the training area. When he walked in the door, though, he was brought up short. Fuck. *Fash.* Fuck.

His hearts rate doubled in incredulity mixed with rage and a twist of lust. Rory was pinned to the ground by one of his lieutenants. The male had her on her stomach, legs spread, as he pinned her with his body asking if she was going to give up. He was preparing to walk over and rip the warrior's head off when Rory slammed her free arm's elbow backwards into the side of the male's head knocking him to the side. She sprang with unbelievable grace and speed to her feet as soon as his weight was displaced and had the warrior pinned in some twisted position he was not sure he could easily duplicate.

His mood was shifting so swiftly he could not keep track of what he was feeling. One moment happy that she got away and appreciative of her skill and the next back to murderous as he caught the fact that the warrior had a perfect view of her ass up close and was leering at it.

He was not the jealous type and the feeling was sitting uncomfortably in his chest, which made him irritable all over again. The original intention of releasing his stress in the training area was a thing of the past. With a loud curse he turned to leave, but Nial must have heard him. His friend called his name from another space in the room. He considered ignoring him, but that would cause his bad mood to spread and that was exactly what he had been trying to avoid while he avoided Rory. He took some deep breaths just as Tarc had taught him, and turned back to Nial, pointedly trying to ignore what was happening with Rory.

"Yes?" That came out almost normal. Or so he thought until he caught Nial's expression. He took another calming breath and in an even more controlled voice, continued. "I see you are training our guests. I hope all is going well."

Nial did not answer right away and he could feel the other male's scrutiny. Satisfied, or ignoring what he saw on Bren's face, he grumbled his response. "Yes. Training has been going relatively well. It should not be necessary as they should still be on Earth, but circumstances being what they are, I believe they are doing a fair job of learning our fighting techniques."

Jill scoffed so loudly he heard her clearly across the space. Rory responded too as she angrily shoved away from the warrior and hissed, "¡Gilipollas!" At least he saw that his warrior was able to untangle his limbs, he supposed he should be grateful for small things.

That lasted only a moment as Nial cursed a streak. The reason for the outburst was a knife quivering and sticking out of the mat right next to his foot. Jill laughed loudly and walked over to the side where Rory now stood near the sharp weapons and the females did the Earth symbol of appreciation with a high-five. Regret coursed through him, briefly, for giving them imbedded translation devices. He did not have time to dwell on it, though, because he heard growling, but only realized it was coming from him after all heads had turned his way.

Before he completely lost his control, he once again turned around and this time stomped out the door. When he made it into the corridor, he expelled a small amount of his tension with a fist into the wall. Fuck that hurt. He was shaking his hand to release some of the pain when he realized he was not alone in the corridor. He turned before his senses could register who and was ready to bite someone's head from their body when he saw her.

She was wearing another tight tank top, this one had a four-letter word across her chest, reading, "Rawr." He was not sure what that meant, but the way the word molded around her breasts made him want to caress every letter. He could not help his eyes roaming down her body to the tight shorts that looked painted on. Her clothes left almost nothing unseen and he had an irrational need to cover her in something very loose. To keep every angle and curve for his eyes only. He reminded himself, unsuccessfully, that he was not a jealous male as his eyes roamed back up her body. His cock was tenting the loose material of his pants and it was clear she noticed as she looked down and her gaze grew hotter. Like a branding caress as they traveled up his nude torso.

He was not sure what to do next. He was ready to push her up against the corridor wall and fuck her no matter who came along and saw. He needed to be inside her. Now. Avoiding her was no longer an option. He was swiftly coming to the conclusion that he would have to pick her up and carry her to his room, when he ran out of choices.

Rory surprisingly jumped across the space separating them— who knew she could jump so far? She had her legs wrapped around his waist, her arms wrapped around his neck, and was licking his throat before he could react. Her tongue was unexpectedly rough, it felt amazing and pushed his need that much higher. *Was she purring?* Then she whispered in his ear, "I need you to fuck me. Right the fuck, now."

That was clear and in complete alignment with his own needs, so he ran. He ran through the corridors with her wrapped tightly around him. It was torture. Her core bounced against his raging cock over and over again. He was going to come while running, something he did not think possible. The female laughed. She actually laughed. Her head was thrown back and she looked as though she was having the ride of her life. He ran harder.

Rory was having the ride of her life. She might well get off just from the amazing dry humping Bren's long, hard length was providing her. And boy was he long and hard. And boy was he getting harder and longer with each bounce. She was quite literally on the verge of orgasm when he stopped moving. "What the fuck? Don't stop now. I was so close." She glared at him and realized he was glaring right back.

"Were you? Now you will have to wait until I give you an orgasm instead of just taking advantage of my body." He humphed at her with indignation.

Who knew he was going to be so stingy with the orgasms? "I wasn't taking advantage of you. I can't help it if your cock and my clit had a fun time playing trampoline." She shrugged.

That was apparently the wrong response because he growled back at her. He growled and then he had her shorts and panties off and his pants down before she could even blink.

"It's a good thing I already know the Staraban have no diseases and, due to your chip, you can't get me pregnant since it seems we're skipping The Talk."

Definitely skipping The Talk. He lifted her against the wall as she spoke, hoisted her legs to his shoulders, bending her in two, and deep dived into her oh-so-wet pussy with one thrust of his hips. She was completely onboard. And full. And moaning. And trying hard not to purr again.

Well, that was true for the initial impalement because then he just stopped moving. His breath was heavy and warm against her neck and he dropped his forehead to her shoulder. She was luckily limber, so she didn't have a problem being folded in half, but just sitting in that position was fucking awkward.

"What the fuck is wrong now? Move your sexy alien ass. You got me here, now work it."

He lifted his head and looked her right in the eyes and gritted out, "I was worried I might have gone too fast and hurt you."

She panted back, "I am a lot stronger than you ever give me credit for. What I can't deal with at this time is my lack of orgasm. Now. Do you plan to remedy that or am I in this position so we can both marvel at my knees?"

Matching a hard thrust to each word, Bren groaned, "You are the most infuriating female. Fine. You want to fuck. We fuck."

And then he began to fuck and it was glorious. He slammed his cock in and out in a rough, jackhammer technique that had her seeing stars. Exciting, mesmerizing stars unlike the ones outside the windows. Her nails, gripping his shoulders, began to elongate again. She was coming apart at the seams. His hard length filling her perfectly over and over and once again she found herself on that sweet, needy precipice.

That was when his rhythm changed. At some point, she couldn't recall exactly when, she must have thrown her head back and closed her eyes, because when he changed things up, her head popped up even as her eyes popped open. She was about to exclaim a giant "what the fuck" again, but his smug stare told her he knew what he'd done and it was entirely deliberate. As she watched him rocking his cock slowly and very deeply into her, he smirked and then shrugged.

Motherfucker had the gall to shrug while stealing another orgasm away from her. She was done playing by his rules. That's it. Rory retracted her nails and used her now free hands, as well as her legs, to push on Bren's shoulders. Hard. His cock left her body as he stumbled backwards and as Rory landed on her feet in a crouch, she swept out her hand and yanked on his ankle, tumbling him to the ground. He landed hard on his back, cursing, but he was a big boy and he was going to be fine. Her poor, overstimulated body, would not be fine if he didn't stop fucking around and instead got down to the business of fucking to completion.

She straddled his hips and slowly sank down on his very erect penis. This position had him even deeper and it was fabulous. Bren looked like he wanted to protest her takeover but as she began her ride of wild abandon, his hands gripped her hips tighter and he matched her thrust for gyration. She fell forward, hands on either side of his head and met his gaze in challenge.

He moved one of his hands from her hips and gripped her head, tangling his fingers in her hair and with firm control, pulled her mouth to his. She liked it. A lot. Her pussy spasmed as his mouth took ownership of hers. His tongue thrust for every thrust of his cock. Wrecking her above and below.

This time when she got close, Rory reared back, put one hand on his beautiful, thick, muscular thigh for support, and trailed her other hand down her stomach where her tank top had ridden up, until she reached her clit. And then she started rubbing it firmly even as she rode wildly. Losing any attempt at a rhythm in her need, she continued until she finally, *finally*, came. Hard.

When her orgasm frenzy finally passed, she looked down to see Bren with his hands behind his head, just staring up at her. He was also clearly still very hard inside her. *Oh shit!* She had never left a lover behind and why the hell was he just lying there looking up at her like a fucking observer. So she asked. "Why the hell are you just lying there? Is this some alien thing I should know about? You have no interest in coming?"

He shrugged. Now she understood why he got so crazed every time she'd done that stupid gesture. What the hell is a shrug supposed to even mean? Before she could berate his inappropriate shrug usage though, he continued. "I was right there with you, but when you started playing with your clit and using my cock like some kind of personal internal massage system, I decided to lay back and enjoy the view. Clearly only one part of me was needed at the time."

She felt her embarrassment from head to toe. Had she really just used him like a vibrator? Yeah. She supposed she had. Wow. That was bitchy even for her. Yet, he didn't actually seem upset about it. "I'm sorry. You're not mad?"

He didn't answer until she found herself pinned beneath all six foot something of him. His thirst-worthy forearms located beside her head as he looked down into her face and said, "I was mad for maybe a second, but you looked so good riding my cock, you felt so good riding my cock, and it was clear I had pushed you to such a height of need that all you could do was ride my cock, so I realized I was okay with that. More than okay. You felt amazing. You looked amazing. And now, I am going to fuck you so hard, it will be amazing if either of us can walk again today."

She gulped because there was no other response to such a pronouncement. Really, there wasn't. Well, except one more. "Give it to me." And he did. He gave it to her hard, fast, and so good, she came again clamping his cock with her spasms as he finally thrust one final time and stiffened above her with his own climax. He called her name as he did, and Rory refused to think about just how good it sounded from his lips. Only later would she acknowledge just how hard she had to fight not to bite him. Not then. She was not going to acknowledge anything except sex between them was at least, no, more explosive than their fights. And that was saying a lot. *¡Joder! She was so fucked!*

Bren could not remember a more exciting and satisfying sexual encounter. He leaned up on his forearms once he caught his breath and looked down at his gorgeous seductress. She had her eyes closed, keeping him from being able to see her unusual, expressive eyes. They reminded him of cat eyes in their color and clarity and he wanted to look into them to get a read on her mood. He took a moment to just savor the feeling of still being inside her wet sheath. He noted that the back of his shoulders hurt, but it was nothing next to the pleasure. She must have some pretty sharp nails. He realized a couple of things just then, actually. His pants were tangled around his feet and her tank top and the earth-torture-device known as a bra, were still on her.

How had he not even touched her breasts? He loved breasts. Adored them even. In fact, he had been eyeing hers earlier and as his gaze took in that four-letter word he had previously been jealous of, he could not help thinking himself an idiot. He could have watched those beauties jiggle the whole time she had ridden him. But, no. Instead, he had been completely distracted with watching her pleasure herself, as well as the pleasure on her features, and failed to address her breasts' unfortunate containment. Apparently, sex with Rory could get better.

Her eyes opened and she studied him. He braced on one arm while bringing the other down to her abdomen. He glided his hand along her body until his fingers snuck under her top. He raised the material as he continued to push his hand across her heated, damp skin. His palm came in contact with the soft cotton material of her jailer.

Then she spoke. "Looking for something?"

"I found something, I would say." He squeezed her breast enjoying the lush feel of her. He wanted to rip everything away and dive face first into her chest. He was growing hard while still inside her with the image of that desire.

"Are you actually growing hard? Again? Already? Still inside me?"

He could think of only one appropriate response. He shrugged. His eyes lifted off of her chest and back to hers in a snap as he heard her chest rumble in clear irritation. Had that really come from her? Was that an Earth female thing? Turning her shrug on her had to be one of the best ideas he had ever had. Instead of answering any of her questions, he chose to bring her with him. He rubbed his thumb over her nipple which he could feel grow erect even through the material of her bra.

Since she raised no protests, he ripped her shirt over her head in a swift movement and then undid the front clasp of her bra the way a human lover he briefly had when they first landed on Earth, taught him. Her breasts were a dream and he their rescuer. They were slightly lighter than the skin on her face and arms but crowned with the most delectable brown nipples. His mouth watered for them. Needed a taste of them.

It had all taken but moments, but he felt as though he had been eye fucking her breasts for ages. Too long. It was time to take that taste. He leaned in and licked the peak of one as he palmed the other. She smelled amazing and tasted even better. A lick was not enough. He enveloped her nipple in his mouth, sucking as he squeezed the other nipple gently between his fingers. He was in breast heaven but even as he grew harder by the acts, he registered that Rory was just, well, lying there.

He lifted his head so he could check in with her and saw that he had been right. She was not unhappy, not wanting to pull away, but just disengaged. That would not work for him in any way.

"Is something wrong?" His voice came out gruff and laden with the control he was exerting to pull back his own lust.

"Not exactly."

"What exactly then?"

"I just am not much of a breast woman. What you are doing feels nice, and pleasurable up to a point but, with nothing else happening, it just doesn't do it for me. I could tell you were enjoying yourself and was looking for a good time to mention it. Now that it has been brought up, please do continue, but do you think you could move your hips and share your attention with other parts of my body?"

Bren had never had a lover be that blatantly honest with him about what they needed and while he wished his enjoyment of her breasts was something they could share equally, with his ability to know what she needed, he was game to spread his focus wider. After all, he found all of her sexy. Including her fierce sexuality and honesty.

"You can have whatever you need. I aim to fuck you wild, so I am glad you told me."

That was the last words either of them said for a while as Bren began to suck her nipple again, but also moved his bracing arm so his hand could grasp her hair firmly, and his other skimmed down her body, down her thigh, and hoisted her leg so her knee was up along his hip. He began to pump into her and for his efforts, Rory began to pant and squirm underneath him. That was much better. Infinitely better.

He was lost tasting her from breast to breast, then up her neck, then indulging in a deep, demanding kiss, and when he felt her nails scratching at his back again, his pleasure doubled knowing she was right there with him. They both came again after a longer, slower, deeper loving and they passed out utterly spent and curled into each other. His last thought was that he would never be able to keep his distance now that he knew, instead of guessed, how it could be with them.

[5]
WHEN THE SHIP BREAKS

Captain's Log: Earth date October 17, 2025

Yeah. That is not going to happen again. Nope.

Rory out.

Captain's Log:Earth date October 19, 2025

Motherfucker.

Rory out.

CHAPTER 5

Staraban Ship, Space

October 17, 2025 Earth Date

Bren woke slowly at the feel of the warm, soft, fuzzy fur as he turned over. He had to assume some of his pets made their way to the bed and joined them as they did most nights. It took him only a moment before he recalled all the ways he and Rory pleasured each other the night before. They had finally made it to his bed during rounds three and four and passed out for a second time late in the night.

He opened his eyes and looked over to his still sleeping companion and froze at the sight. Rory was curled on her side and every single cat he had adopted while still on Earth surrounded her. They were curled up against her instead of him and she looked as though she was perfectly comfortable. Almost like she was one of them. Just another warm lump of cuteness curled into another. The comparison seemed especially apt since Rory, like his feline friends, hid her dangerous, sharp, killer edge under all that seeming adorableness.

It was still a bit of a surprise and, he had to admit, hurt a bit, that none of his cats had made their way over to cuddle with him. He was the one that had provided for them since taking them in. One night, and they turned traitor. He had learned quickly that you do not dislodge a happy cat, so he tried to get out of the bed without waking any of them. That was when everything went very wrong.

Apparently, Rory was a light sleeper ready for a brawl because as he began to roll out of the bed, she jumped up into a crouch—naked, stunning, and deranged. That was not the biggest problem though. Her alarm and sudden movement sent all fifteen of his cats jumping and screeching, claws bared in all directions including his. A couple of them latched on to his chest as he reflexively protected his cock. He cringed in pain but otherwise, tried to suppress his instinct to scream lest he scare them even more. When they all settled, he gently plucked off the two dangling from him and placed them on the ground. He stood up again and looked Rory directly in the eyes, assuming he would see sympathy or regret. What he saw instead, even as the gouges in his skin ran with tiny rivulets of blood, was a female on the verge of laughter.

"You are evil, female."

She lost her fight and collapsed on the bed convulsing with her mirth. He was too shocked to move for all of the span of a set of his heartbeats and then he pounced himself. And tickled her.

"Find this funny, do you? I am mortally wounded by flying feline knives. How dare you? Now you will have to beg for my mercy. And I do not have any."

She attempted to dislodge him but was laughing too hard and was barely able to draw breath. She finally squeaked out, "¡Dios santo! Mercy!"

He relented and watched as she gasped deep, heaving breaths. He collapsed back on the bed lying down next to her head and stared up at the ceiling, a common position for him lately, trying to understand how his morning had gotten so confusing. Oh yeah. He was dealing with *her*. The female who had been his tormentor from the day they met.

She moved, and he felt her tongue on his abdomen even as he felt the silk of her hair caress across his chest. What was she up to now? Whatever it was, he would let her. Damn him. He was so easy. Her tongue made its way to his navel and then down to the notch where his abdomen met his hips and then—Was she going to?—Oh yes. Yes she was. She licked his hardening erection from root to tip. Oh Goddess. She rolled her tongue around the bulbus end licking up the precum he was sure his body must be leaking in his burgeoning excitement. It felt debilitatingly good.

She continued working her tongue all around, up and down, teasing him to harden ever more. Then she snaked her hand between his legs and began playing with his balls with her fingers. *Fash!* He almost came right then and there. He held back, though, hands fisted at his sides.

Her body shifted and next thing he knew, he had her wet, needy pussy hovering right above his face as she straddled him. Then it was no longer hovering but was placed square against his mouth and nose, smothering him. Of course, that was the moment he needed air the most as her mouth also engulfed his cock completely. She might well be trying to kill him, but he could not bring himself to care. Death by vagina smothering seemed like a reasonable way to go. Warriors would call him a lucky *sharta*.

Eventually, from sheer preservation, using his hands on her hips, he shifted them up just a little so he could breathe as well as pleasure her back. He used his fingers to open her up and began to lick. She overwhelmed all of his senses.

As she began purring along the whole length of his cock, he thought he might die yet, from pleasure this time. If it was his time, it was his time. He kept licking at her labia, her clit, and then diving his tongue as deep as it could go into her sex. She smelled and tasted like Rory and sex and something else that he could not quite place but that was very pleasing to him.

As he continued, so did she. She pumped her head up and down along his cock sucking and licking and grazing her teeth ever so gently. He was so close. So damn close. He could feel as his balls drew up closer to his body, straining for release, but he refused to do so, until she came first. He plunged two fingers into her as his tongue flicked a furious rhythm against her hard clit until he heard her mouth come off his cock with a pop and she gasped and moaned coming all over his chin. He grinned in satisfaction which lasted only a moment as she took him in her mouth again so deep he felt the back of her throat and then she hummed and his balls rolled up into his head, oh wait… his eyes into his head, his balls… whatever. He grew taut and came down her throat as she greedily swallowed everything he gave her. Fuck.

"Fuck."

"Oral."

"Uh huh."

He was as limp as a cat in the sun.

Rory, on the other hand, jumped off of him in a burst of energy and motion.

He lifted his head. "Where are you going?"

"To get the day started, of course. I have things to do. Thanks for the great night."

With that she walked into his cleaning room, came out five minutes later, threw her clothes on, waved and was out his door. He was the ship's commander. He had things he had to do too, but he found himself lying in bed looking at his ceiling wondering how his life had gotten so out of his control and when could he get his hands on her again.

Two days later…

"¡Coño!" Rory hissed between her teeth in frustration. This was her fourth attempt to relieve her sexual frustration in the last couple of days and all she'd accomplished was to edge herself. Seriously. Since when couldn't she give herself relief? She was quite proficient at it, but just when she thought she was going to fall over that blissful edge, an image of Bren's disappointed-growing-to-irate face would cross her imaginings and… nothing. Like a popped balloon all her pleasure would whoosh out of her every pore. She was not going to cave though. No way.

She couldn't—no, she needed to be honest with herself—*wouldn't* risk jumping back into bed with him. Rory had her reasons for her many casual liaisons and while her bed gymnastics with Bren ranked up there as, well, the best ever by a significant margin, she wasn't about to go back for seconds. Not if she could help it. In fact, the more she wanted to, the more she resolved not to.

That didn't make life in close quarters with the object of her obsession and consternation any easier. It was clear to her that since realizing she planned to avoid any more bumps and grinds, Bren had made it his business to bump into her everywhere she went and that had her grinding her teeth at every such encounter. Despite all her efforts, she wanted him. Wanted his body, his tongue, his taste, his cock, and even his fucking cats. That had been the best night of sleep she'd had since boarding his stupid ship.

"¡Joder!" Her expression of annoyance didn't lesson her frustration one bit and neither did the pain spreading through the toe she grabbed on to after having kicked the wall in the cleaning room. Fuck it. She was going to go train and if he found her there, all the better. She would just beat the crap out of him, figuratively, and get it out of her system.

As she dressed, she turned flushed with embarrassment because that was the moment Hal decided to remind her he was still turned on, much like her, but not in the same way.

"I don't understand what your problem is. Why wouldn't you jump your hunky alien? I mean, he isn't my Will, but he is still quite yummy." At the mention of Hal's perpetual crush, her friend Will, she briefly wondered how his transition to being a vampire was going. Then she remembered what else Hal said and cringed.

"¡Mierda! I guess you've been here the whole time as I—"

"Oh, yes."

"Why didn't you say anything? Perv."

"And break your concentration? No way. You've been a real shit to work with the last couple of days. I was cheering you on."

"I can't believe you just said that."

"I'm a very supportive type of PAL, you know."

She snorted at that. He had been such a pain in the ass to her friend Jack before the transfer and now she understood why her friend had loved and yet bemoaned him.

"How about you never mention any of this ever again and we both forget it happened?"

"I could do that. I won't. But I could."

"Ass."

"I find that offensive."

"I find this conversation offensive. Go fuck yourself."

"Rude! But I bet I'd do a better job of it than you just did."

Rory was sorely tempted to punch herself in her own head since that was where he was installed. That didn't seem like a wise decision though. She finished dressing in her black tank and shorts and responded, "I think it's time for you to have a long, looonnggg, slee—"

She was startled into silence at the first explosive sound even as the ship shook around them.

"Fuck!" They said in unison. She strapped a holster belt, with her gun and clips, around her waist, her throwing knives around one thigh, another knife around the other, and one more around her ankle. She also put on her newly-made double back harness for the wicked dual alien blades she'd decided to adopt. She ran out the door as another explosion shook the ship.

She had just made it to the bridge when a fourth explosion hit. Along the way, announcements had been made, so she knew they were under attack and that everyone was manning their defense and attack stations. She took in the bridge at a glance. The clear swivel chairs that popped out of the floor at every station were full. On the screen was a ship with the image of lasers shooting before another explosion rocked them. Bren stood in the center of the space issuing commands like a leader.

Not *like* a leader, he *was* the leader.

Pues claro. It was a side she hadn't really seen before and frankly hadn't ever given him the credit he was due. He looked hot. If they weren't in the middle of a fight in space, she would have been tempted to jump him right then. But they were. She looked around and didn't see Nial or Jill. *Shit.*

She caught Bren's concerned face as he turned to her and watched as it turned darker still. Before he had a chance to tell her to go hide or something similarly angering and idiotic, she sent him an air kiss, turned and ran out. In the corridors where there was no one else, she used the bonus of her cat speed and within moments made it to the training room. No Nial or Jill here either. She assumed Nial might be leading those manning the ship's weapons, but where was Jill?

She continued running through the ship even as another explosion rocked it. This time, so hard, it slammed her against the wall of the corridor. "Fuck! That one hurt." It did work to get her brain back online so instead of running off, she asked, "Hal, can you find where Jill is?"

"I was wondering where you were going in such a rush. Yes. Give me just a minut—oh—Jill is in the medical center. Why would she be there?"

She took off toward that part of the ship and arrived soon after only to find Jill lying on one of the medical beds with the Staraban version of a doctor working over her. "What happened?"

The doctor never looked up, but answered, "She was testing a set of sharp weapons when the ship was attacked and she was sliced multiple times by the falling weapons. Worse, she fell onto the weapon she had in her hand and that wound is quite deep. She should live, but it's going to take some time to repair the damage."

An eerie silence fell over the room, the ship, the universe as far as she could tell. Everything held its breath. Bren's voice came over the intercom system. "The Vrolan attack ship has been defeated. Thank you all for your fast reactions. I need a damage assessment as soon as possible. *Adrana.*" Rory recognized the Staraban word, which was good job, appreciation, and respect all rolled into one.

She was about to inquire about Jill again, when she heard footsteps coming fast from the hallway. Nial was in the doorway a moment later, concern clear on his features. "How is she?"

The doctor answered, "Like I told this human female, she is

stable, but there is a lot of repair needed. She will live. You were wise to bring her in quickly, though. I am concerned about her blood loss. The doctor finally looked up at Rory. "Could you donate some blood if necessary? I know not all humans are compatible on Earth, but we have a way of circumventing that."

Rory wanted to answer in the positive instantly, but knowing what that could mean, she hesitated. Still, if there was no other choice, "Yes." She nodded in the affirmative as well, firming her decision within herself. She turned again to Nial. "You brought her in?"

His jaw firmed but he controlled any other reaction. "Yes. We were training on weapons when the ship was attacked. I should never have allowed her access to the weapons. What was I thinking?" The last couple of sentences he said while looking at the ground and as though to himself.

Her feminist blood boiled. "Oh. No. You. Don't. Jill is a fighter and you can't take that from her. Just like I am. Fighters get hurt. It happens. Though, if she does survive, I plan on giving her so much shit for stabbing herself." Nial blanched at her in shock, which just made her… shrug. The big, bad warrior looked like she'd offended his delicate sensibilities. He was going to clutch his pearls next. *Sheesh!* "Cálmate."

She assessed the room. There was nothing useful she could do there. "Let me know if you need me to come in and provide my blood. I'm going to check on the damage. I should be able to help with the repairs."

The doctor nodded slightly but mostly just continued to go about putting her friend back together. As she passed Nial, he grunted at her then mumbled under his breath, "As though Bren would let you help with that."

Her back stiffened, but she wouldn't judge Bren on what his friend said. She'd wait for him to do something wrong before she began throwing her knives again.

Minutes later, she was in the main engine room throwing a knife over Bren's unflinching shoulder. It thwacked irately into the metal wall behind him. Rory thundered. "What did you just say to me?"

"Do you settle all your disagreements by throwing a knife?" Bren responded nonchalantly.

"No. Sometimes I use my gun."

He did not doubt it. Why did he want this woman so badly? He only had to look as far as her newest tight black tank top with the word "Hiss" across her crave-inducing breasts to remember exactly why. Well, that and the passion she displayed in everything she did. Her flame was like the brightest of suns and if you got too close, you *would* get burned, but Goddess, it was magnificent. She was magnificent. Memories of the way she flamed so hot in her desire with him kept Bren wanting.

Wanting.

And waiting.

And missing.

And wondering.

And fucking confused.

And angry.

So *fashing* angry. He had walked into engineering to get an assessment of the damages only to find her there. Behaving like she was a part of the crew. His crew. His anger eclipsed his reason. She was not a part of his crew. And after the attack they just survived, with her in danger she should never have been in… Would never have been in if she had stayed on Earth where he had left her. Oh yeah. He was definitely angry. In fact, if she had never come, he would not have learned what he was now missing. Experienced the heights and now depths she brought out in him. Oh. He was angry alright, but also highly resentful. Somewhere, behind it all lay another emotion he refused to examine… fear.

He swiftly shut down that avenue of thinking. In an attempt to avoid all distractions, he decided the only way forward was to compartmentalize. He would ignore all else except what he needed to do to fix his ship and take care of his crew, which included getting her out of the way. "If you do not return to your room, I will have my warriors escort you."

There was a moment when her hard face seemed to soften with hurt, but he might have imagined it because it hardened with a chilling calm before she turned on her heel and strode away yelling over her shoulder, "Misogynistic ass!" The breath he had been holding, in anticipation of her next attack, whooshed out of his burning lungs upon her retreat. *Well, fash.*

He felt completely drained by everything and there was an unexplainable tightness around his hearts, but there was nothing he could do except what needed to be done. He proceeded to check in with the engineering crew. Some minor damages but they would know more in a few hours. He moved on and made sure to connect with each of his team leaders to learn that injuries were few and far between, a testament to how well trained his crew was. It was exhausting work to be the confidant and encouraging commander for his warriors even as his body felt the drop of his adrenaline rush of earlier. He would not let them down, though.

He still had one more visit. He found Nial exactly where he thought he would, at Jill's side. He had left this visit for last because he had been studiously avoiding thinking about Rory. As he entered and saw Jill laying on a medical bed, unconscious and covered in bandages and medical devices, his mind went exactly where he knew it would. He pictured Rory the same and he was once again thrown back into the blazing anger of before. If the two females had not come, Jill would not be injured. They would both be safe.

He suppressed his feelings back down because his friend was going to need him too. "How is she?" He turned toward Nial as he spoke. The warrior's face was blank, but Bren knew a mask when he saw one.

"She has quite a few minor cuts but it is one severe stab wound to the gut that has caused her to lose a lot of blood, as well as damaging her insides. The machines are trying to patch up her body, so Batan has put her into a medical sleep so she may stay calm and heal."

Bren put a hand on his friend's shoulder and squeezed. "Do you need anything?"

"Why would I need anything?" In contradiction to his words,

Bren felt the tension coursing through his friend where his hand made contact.

"Because we both know that despite your claims to the contrary, you care for this human."

"Who would be stupid enough to care for one of these ridiculously breakable species?" Nial shrugged off his hand and walked away a few steps. Then he turned back and met Bren's eyes. He said nothing more, but Bren could read it all from that one look.

He shot Nial a return look that acknowledged they were both exactly that amount of stupid.

Nial asked, "Since I do not see her here, can I assume at least Rory is unharmed? I saw her when I first arrived but she rushed out relatively quickly. Nothing happened to her since then?"

"No."

"Then why do you look ready to do violence? And do not try to lie to me. I see your mask, and what you are trying to hide behind it, my friend. I have also seen what you have been like since that day you stormed out of the training room. What is happening with you?"

Bren sighed with his whole being. Why was he so turbulent? He knew even if he did not like to admit to it. "I came here to check on you but you are turning it on me instead." He considered where to start. "Have you ever thought about why I freely have relations with so many without ever considering more than some shared pleasure?"

"This is not the conversation I expected to be having, but now that you mention it, no. It has always just been your way. I now see that none of us, as far as I know, have ever asked you about it."

"No. You have not." Nial walked back closer to him. Lending strength? Creating a more intimate setting? He was not sure the reason, but he appreciated the gesture.

Nial quietly asked, "Then, why?"

"I have never really discussed this before because I thought no one else would understand. Everyone else seemed okay with dating and trying out relationships with different people to see if they fit. The thing is, Nial, from the day I first took notice of having a sexual attraction to anyone, I also took note that I had nothing but sexual attraction. That my feelings were not engaged at all. I was ready to share pleasure and that was it. It never felt like experiencing more was out of the realm of possibility, I just had not found anyone I wanted more with. Not one person and you know I have been around the universe enjoying many mutually enjoyed encounters."

"And now is different?"

He took a shuddering breath and a smile tugged at his lips just thinking of her. "Rory walked into my life that first day and the only thing I wanted to do was hold her against me and never let her go. It was the most exciting and scariest thing I had ever felt."

"Despite the fact that I *have* been in a few relationships in the past, I think I know exactly what you mean." His friend looked over to Jill as he spoke with a look Bren could only call pure hunger on his face before he shut it down.

"Yeah. I have a feeling Tarc was in our same predicament with Jack. A lot of his actions make more sense to me now."

"Definitely. What will you do next?"

"I have no idea, but I need to rest. I can do that here if you would like me to stay with you."

"No. I am just going to grab a chair and check in with some of my teams. You should go get some sleep. I wish neither of them were here and yet, I have enjoyed having her here."

"I feel the same way. I will be in my room if you need me." He patted Nial on the back one last time as he walked out.

He could not stay this emotionally unstable. There was no way he could function properly as commander if he did. Having dispensed all the necessary orders and ensured repairs were under-way, he retreated to his room. He sat on his couch and within moments, he was stroking the cats that came to comfort him even as he leaned his head back and closed his eyes. What was he going to do now? They needed to divert to the nearest AAA-affiliated colony for repairs. Maybe it would be safer to put the females into a pris-oner cell, but he would be deluding himself if he thought he could actually do that.

He wished to have Rory safe and willing to compromise, but not to break her spirit or tame her. As with his cats, they were fierce and needed their freedom and space. He could not take that from her. Her fierce spirit was one of the things he liked most about her. Somehow, he would have to find a way to keep her safe. Goddess only knew how he would accomplish it. He also had to find a way for them to work together. Knives and harsh decrees would get them nowhere. And how could he convince her to come back to his bed? Bren fell fast asleep thinking about tasty breasts. And…silky fur?

Rory fumed for a while. How long? Who knew? Who cared? Between her upbringing surrounded by the fiery, life-embracing nature of her Gitano people, the passionate nature of Andalusia, and her grudge-keeping cat nature, well, it took some time. She had no illusions of herself. She was as loyal as the day was long, but she also ran hot when her hackles were triggered and nothing triggered her more than someone, especially a man, trying to control her.

Then, all bets were off.

It was why she'd run away from her people and why she kept her distance rather than forming relationships. It was why she'd built a fortress around her heart which kept almost everyone else out. It was why she could never go home and why she trained in munitions and fighting skills. It was why she would never allow herself to fall under another man's control.

Never again.

And now, to have this guy, this alien, attempt to control her while also playing center stage in all her fantasies? Well… that was making her fuse shorter than usual.

Eventually, she did calm down and had to acknowledge that while he had been inappropriate and sexist in wanting her to go to her room like a child, answering him with throwing knives hadn't been her finest hour and may have, perhaps, just a little, seemed a tiny bit like a childish response. Maybe.

What had been clear to her as he entered the fray, was that he was upset from the get-go. Had he seen Jill? Was that the problem?

Or maybe just thinking about the attack was upsetting him? Definitely, something had and it explained why he reverted back to being overprotective.

They needed to talk. Damn. She hated having to apologize, but she thought perhaps they both were in the wrong in this last exchange.

She went in search of him and found him in his room. Asleep. She was actually a little surprised he hadn't heard her knocking, but Hal had assured her that she would find her "aggravating man candy," his words not hers, in this room. When he hadn't responded, she grew concerned and had Hal open the door for her. She stepped in and stood rooted in place, staring at the sight that greeted her.

Her big, bad, commanding warrior was passed out asleep sitting up on his couch while his cats curled up around him from all sides. He looked like he was wearing a long fur coat. Her human side thought it was the most adorable thing she'd ever seen. Her cat nature, well, that was another story. Her cat side was ready to snap and hiss and claw all the little furballs to pieces for invading her territory. Since when had she started thinking of Bren as her anything?

Instinct being what it was, she went with the hissing. It only took one hiss and the other felines, with much tail twitching and resentful whisker flicking, moved away. Bren still hadn't stirred. He looked absolutely delicious and she let her gaze devour him in a way she hadn't allowed herself these last few days. Memories of his firm hands, warm mouth, and delicious cock swam through her mind. Thinking of his cock as delicious made her mouth water. There are many ways to apologize, but an apology of action seemed more appealing to her by the second.

She kneeled between his spread legs and considered her actions. She didn't want to violate him, but considering the looks he'd been sending her way the last couple of days, she felt confident in her welcome. Still, she paused. As she watched, his cock began twitching beneath his uniform and he mumbled, "Rory," with a soft groan.

Okay. Clearly, she had a starring role in his sexy dream. Good sign she'd be welcome. She'd stop at the first sign of his discontent. Resolved, she carefully began to rub the slight bulge at the juncture of his legs. It grew even more as she caressed him. And hardened as she rubbed her cheek along the length.

"Are you planning on torturing me now instead of throwing knives?"

Rory startled, then looked at his face. His eyes were staring down into hers. She answered huskily, "No. No knives. Take your uniform off."

"I thought you were avoiding me."

"I was."

"What changed?"

"Me. Now take your uniform off."

He didn't comply right away but just considered her. She wasn't sure what she would do if he rejected her. She sat immobile waiting for his response. Finally, he began taking his uniform off. He ripped the top apart, closures flying everywhere. He lifted his hips up as he pushed the material down toward his thighs. That was as far as he got before she decided she'd had enough waiting.

She grabbed his hands and moved them to the side of his thighs as she leaned in and licked his newly revealed shaft, jutting straight up toward his stomach, from balls to tip. His deep groan spread a heated delight through her whole being. Still holding his hands to the couch, she used just her mouth on him leaving a trail of licks and kisses along his golden length. Up one side and down the other. She felt the tension in the fisted hands she gripped and felt her own sexual power in the moment.

She swirled her tongue around his tip, licking up the escaped precum and heard his breathing grow ragged.

He practically growled at her. "Give me your mouth, female."

"With that attitude? I need to consider my options—"

"Please. Rory. Stop teasing me. I have been miserable in my need for you for days."

Music to her ears. She was not the only one who had been miserable with her imposed distance. There were a lot of good reasons for that distance, but right then, she couldn't think of one. And he *had* said please.

She took part of his length fully into her mouth making him gasp, his hips jerking a little pushing him a little further in.

"Oh Goddess, Rory."

She pulled back to get some air and then sank down even deeper on his cock while sucking. She repeated the movement, going a little further down on his length with each pass until she had most of him spreading her lips and down her throat. She purred in enjoyment. The rumbling vibrated her throat and mouth around him and she tasted more precum.

His breathing was labored and under her hands, his were like iron fists. She hung there letting the tension escalate between them, threaded with expectation for what would happen next. She didn't have long to wait. Bren moved so fast and unexpectedly, that she found herself sitting in his lap facing away. He had her shorts and underwear down to her thighs, trapping her legs together.

She panted in anticipation. He was so strong. The human partners she had been with might never have realized it, but she had always been the stronger one in any coupling. With Bren it would be a toss-up, too close to call, and it revved her engine to dangerous levels. She had a momentary twinge of doubt creep in because that was why she was keeping her distance in the first place. It was too good. Too much to handle to stay in control.

Then he cupped her pussy, wet and ready for him, and she wasn't going anywhere but down. Down onto his hard length, which felt all that much bigger for having her legs locked together. She couldn't contain the low, guttural groan that escaped her as every thick, hard inch of him entered her swollen core.

"You feel so big. So fucking big like this."

"And you feel even tighter. Like you are choking my cock."

As his cock slowly disappeared inch by inch into her, his hand played with her folds. Spreading them wide and then grazing past her clit. Her need escalated nearer, ever nearer to a full-on frenzy. But not quite getting there. Well, dammit! If she didn't want to get all the way there, she could have continued to masturbate.

She needed more contact for her clit, so she swiftly bent in half and pushed her shorts down to her ankles, unhooking one, and spread her legs as wide as she could. Then she began rolling her hips, which had the added benefit of forcing his roving hand to do more than lightly touch but instead bump into her needy clit. He yanked her tank and bra down exposing one breast, which he swiftly gripped and pinched. Hard.

"Ow!"

"Behave."

She took that as an invitation to move faster, because fuck no, she would never behave. Also, she liked it. Clearly there was some breast play she did enjoy. She needed it rougher and done while as sensitive as she was at that moment, because it definitely worked for her now.

"Ow! ¡Cabrón!" He'd pinched her again and then rolled his fingers and it hurt. And it felt exquisite. And it made her even wilder so she began to rock her hips even harder still as her own hand slid down to join his in rubbing her clit. She quickly learned he didn't appreciate the intervention because she found her hand pushed out of the way and then the bastard slapped her clit.

"Ah! ¡Ay! ¡Dios! ¡Mío!" She hadn't been prepared for it, nor for how she reacted. It hurt, but it also brought a wave of pleasure in its wake. She was ready for another. "Give it to me again. Please."

"You deserve nothing less than some slaps for avoiding me the last few days and for throwing knives at me at every turn and for calling me names—"

It seemed like he was going to keep talking, and there was plenty to say, but she wanted none of it, so she maneuvered her hand back toward her clit, and before she got there...*Slap*! Oh, yeah. The momentary pain and release caused her whole body to quake. Her head was pulled back roughly by the hand she hadn't noticed abandoning her breast. He was definitely as strong as he seemed and fuck, she was such a goner for him. He was controlling her like his own little sex kitten and all she wanted to do was continue to purr. Dangerous. He was so dangerous. Later, she would worry about it again. Right then, he could pretty much have anything he wanted.

Slap! Slap! Slap!

"¡Ay! ¡Ay! ¡Ay!"

She was so damn close. Coiled like a hammer waiting for the slightest touch on the trigger and ready to strike in an orgasmic explosion. Just a little more. She needed just a little more, but he moved his hand away and a whimper spilled from her lips. A sound she couldn't remember ever having made before.

"Please. Please." And now she was begging. Not the sexy play acting at begging but honest, needy, desperate, embarrassing, but necessary begging. She needed him so badly. She'd missed him so much.

No.

She'd missed his body.

That's all.

But it didn't matter how she labeled it. Right then, she needed and yet she could feel him drawing back even as he held firm to her hair. The words came out as a plea.

"Please. Please don't stop."

Her need clawed her insides raw. Some days, it didn't pay to have the instincts of a cat. Those mating instincts were now leaving claw marks on her heart—no, dammit—just her libido. She would not acknowledge anything else. Whatever part of her was being exposed and laid bare, the only solution was an orgasm from him, *with* him. She whimpered, "Por favor. Dámelo todo."

[6]

THE MARKET ZONE

Captain's Log: Earth date October 19, 2025

Well, fuck. Literally and figuratively.

Rory out.

Captain's Log: Earth date October 21, 2025

Space port shopping is something I can get behind. Especially tech shopping. First I need to figure out some currency and a way to get past Bren's decree that I don't leave the ship. When will he figure out I won't be controlled? Ever. Is being this dense an alien thing? I will not be manipulated by my libido either. Space is my new frontier and I plan to indulge in it with my whole being. Estoy lista. ¡Vamos!

. . .

Rory out.

CHAPTER 6

Staraban Ship, Space

October 19, 2025 Earth Date

"Please, Bren."

Rory was begging so sweetly, but he needed some assurances. He did not plan to allow her to use him and ignore him at her whim. If nothing else, his talk earlier with Nial helped him clarify some of what he was feeling about her. He might have been fine with casual in his past. Had been all about a good fucking and then making a swift exit. He never played at wanting anything else, and his lovers did not expect anything more either. But this female, she was different. He wanted different things with her. He was not sure what, but he had hated the last few days of being ignored. Hated it. And he was not going to be handled by her in that way.

Finding her on her knees caressing him had been both wonderful and angering. Given, neither of them had made any promises, but the night and morning they had shared with each other had been so much more than just sex.

At least he thought so.

He wanted to punish her for denying him—denying them—these last couple of days. But did he have the right? They really had not promised each other anything. This time, he planned to have an understanding before they went any further. He owed her a response to her pleading, but it was not going to be the one she wanted.

"What are you doing here, Rory?"

"¿Qué? Isn't it obvious? I'm currently impaled on your cock. Isn't that self-explanatory?"

Exasperating woman. Her voice was strained, she sounded at her wits' end, and yet she was still being obtuse. He doubted she could hold out for too much longer, though. Maybe he *would* get some honesty from her.

"I refuse to be a plaything that you use and discard at your whim. You will promise me there will be no more avoiding me or we are done here."

"What? Do you really want to stop?"

His anger rose and he had not planned it, but his grip on her hair firmed. Her breath caught and her eyes closed. Clearly she enjoyed when he was rough with her. Good. He wanted to be rough with her. He wanted to enjoy every part of her. The gentle, the wild, the angry, and the soft purring kitten. He wanted every piece of her and he was done questioning it. It was what it was. That was all he needed to know.

"I can stop because I will not be used by you. Now promise me. No more distance."

She seemed torn. On the verge of giving them both what they wanted but with something holding her back. He was not above giving her a nudge over. He rubbed his nose along the length of her exposed neck as his free hand moved up the length of her thigh toward where their bodies were joined. "Tell me what I want to hear. What we both want to happen. Even if your mind is unsure, your body knows we are not finished with each other. We have been at this dance since day one. Is it not time for us to see what happens when we give in?"

A shudder ran through her and she angrily shot back, "Fine! Damn you. No more distance. You happy?"

"I will be and so will you."

He slapped her clit again. Her exhalation of air followed by her body melting into his confirmed what he had just said. He ran his teeth along her throat as his fingers began to play with her clit with purpose. It amazed him just how in-tune his body was to her every reaction. As if her energy spoke to his. He could tell, for instance, the moment her passion was back on the rise. The moment she was back to being close to her release. And in that moment, he knew that one more slap would throw her right over. Having such knowledge and control over this fiercely independent and proud female was causing his hold over his own need to fracture. And he'd been right.

One slap, and her body shook with her pleasure and squeezed his cock so perfectly. She collapsed back on him and he was done in. He flipped her forward, momentarily exiting her body, and proceeded to lay her over the low, glass table in front of the couch. He slid to his knees and reentered her with a hard thrust. Her gasp as her chest with one exposed breast connected with the glass made him smile knowing the cold would wake her back up from her languid aftermath. Her even bigger gasp as he entered her sweet heat, would do the trick too. He ran a hand along her back from her neck down to the juncture with her gorgeous butt.

"Is your nipple enjoying my table?"

"¡Cállate! Fuck me or fuck off."

"Still ready for a fight? Let us see if I can fuck you back to purring."

He firmed his hand on her back applying pressure to keep her down, while with his other he grabbed on to her hip as he began a slow glide in and out of her tight, wet sheath. Still in his moment of knowing, and since she wanted a fast, hard fucking, he deliberately kept a slow pace. Her breathing hitched at his first deep thrust, but when she caught on to his deliberate rhythm, he could swear she hissed.

"What are you doing back there? You call this fucking?"

"I call this my time. I thought you did not want any more talking."

The glower she sent him over her shoulder made him chuckle. He was willing to share control, but not now. Right now, he was in charge, and she was going to just have to come to terms with not getting her way.

"You feel amazing, *Makari*. I could stay right here for hours."

"Who has that kind of time?"

He laughed. "Fair point. Perhaps the next thirty minutes then."

"Bren!"

"Yes, Rory?" He continued with his easy, lazy thrusts even as his dick wanted to join in her rebellion. "Do recall I was pleased to lay there as you enjoyed my body the other day at your pace. I enjoyed the view and providing you with pleasure. All I want is for you to do the same now. Give me this, *Markari*."

It looked as though she was debating with herself as she opened her mouth, closed it, opened it, closed it, and finally put her forehead to the table and whimpered. "Fair. I'm yours tonight, guapo mío."

The feeling of possession, of affection swarmed him. He knew she did not have to give in. She could have easily said no and he would have let her go. She could have fought because she wanted to keep things at that confrontational level. There were many ways she could have responded and this complete surrender nearly undid him.

He kissed up her spine until he nuzzled her neck and whispered, "Thank you," directly into her ear, before biting her lobe and flexing his hips at the same time. Her moan of pleasure followed by a clench of her inner walls nearly drove him past his own control. He wrapped his hand in her hair turning her lips to his and devoured her mouth before releasing her and leaning back to kneeling.

"Tell me again what you need."

Her voice was low, and needy as she replied, "Por favor. I need you to move. I can't take this anymore. Te necesito."

"Such sweet words. You shall have me. All of me is yours, *Makari*."

He braced both hands on her rounded hips and thrust, seating himself deep within her cunt, and then began to build up speed until he was pounding into her so relentlessly, their bodies made the most wonderfully obscene wet sounds. His control was fraying and he wanted to feel her come on him again. He snaked a hand around her neck and with a firm hold, held her arched off the table. His other hand moved to the front of her pussy, found her hard nub, and began to vigorously rub her to climax.

She was roughly panting and her hips pushed back in an opposite rhythm, meeting his thrust-for-thrust. Rory had too much energy in her to sit still for long. Moments later, she yelled out his name even as her body shook all over and her sweet cunt quivered as wetness coated his cock. He was undone. He moved both hands back to her hips and a few brutal thrusts later, he found his own release. He wanted to just fall upon her in his satisfaction, but not on the table, so he wrapped his arms around her middle, and threw them both back onto the couch. Then he just held her collapsed against him as their breathing came back to normal.

Contentment could not fully describe how he felt holding her right then. A part of him worried that perhaps he pushed her too hard, too fast and despite her promise, she would find a way to put distance between them, but he did not dwell on it as they drifted together.

What the fuck did I agree to?

This was not the first time Rory had asked herself that in her lifetime, but it *was* the first time she had thought it about a potential relationship. There were not supposed to be any relationships. Bren's pussy slap interrogation technique had to be a violation of something. Okay. She had agreed not to avoid him. Was that *really* a relationship? So…it's fine. Since a couple of days ago, when she had made her promise under pleasurable duress, they had come together like phosphorous and a match. Combustible.

So… Recurring fuck buddies. She could handle that. It didn't have to mean anything more than they were going to enjoy each other while they were on this ship. When she got back to Earth, she would go on with her normally scheduled sex-a-palooza. And, really, that assumed they didn't tire of each other before then. Surely, it wouldn't last that long. Not with the way they were going at it. Flames that burn hot, burn out or some such shit.

Comforted by her rationalizations, Rory continued down the corridor toward the medical room. She had been visiting every day, and every time she ran into the same doctor alien as that first day.

"How's Jill today?"

The alien looked up with surprise since Rory didn't usually make any sound when she moved unless she remembered to do so on purpose.

"Sorry to startle you."

The alien nodded in acknowledgment. "Still the same. She is holding strong, but I want to keep her sedated a little bit longer to give her body a chance to heal a little bit more."

"That is probably a good idea. I bet if she was awake, it would be a struggle to keep her here."

"Yes. That is what Nial thought as well."

"He's been by to visit?"

"Yes. He sleeps here every night."

¡Qué interesante! If Jill were awake she would have a few choice words for the guy, but it was clear he cared for her friend despite always getting into screaming matches with her. All she said to the good doctor, though, was, "I see. I think we are past due for an introduction. I'm Rory."

"I am called Batan."

"Thank you for taking good care of my friend, Batan. How long do you think she will need to stay under?"

"Maybe a few hours, maybe one more day. She has been healing swiftly, but there are certain markers I want to check off before rousing her."

"Great. Could you let me know if anything changes?"

"Yes."

"Okay. I will go make myself useful then." Rory turned and walked back out. Batan was a female of few words. She could appreciate that. She couldn't emulate that, but she could appreciate it. As soon as she stepped outside, Rory took a deep breath. She was concerned for her new friend, but Jill really did seem stable and healing so other than to wait, there was nothing more Rory could do for her. She just thanked her lucky stars that Jill didn't end up needing any of her blood. That could have brought up uncomfortable questions and side effects. Even with all this stability, Rory would be a lot more relaxed once Jill opened her eyes and was her old, touchy, foul-mouthed self. She missed all of that about her.

What to do next? She decided to investigate the armory. When she reached the room, she found it full of warriors. Well, not exactly full, but there were a few warriors still reinstalling some of the weapons that had fallen down or been damaged during the attack. The last couple of days there had only been one or two she had worked with repairing the weapons, but apparently a bigger group was assigned to set the room to rights. While you still couldn't say it was a huge group, you could say they were huge and that made it seem awfully crowded. Too crowded. Not the armory then. *Engineering here I come.*

After days of traversing the ship as a panther with Hal's help, she had learned her way around quite well. Thinking of Hal, she realized she hadn't talked to him since the day before. She touched behind her ear and mentally thought at him. "Hey. Hal."

He thought back at her, "I understand now why the genies in the bottle were always complaining. Do you know how boring it is to be asleep for so long?"

"Now that you mention it, I guess not. Isn't it like real sleeping? Are you telling me you are aware when you are asleep?"

"I didn't used to be, but I was built to evolve. To learn. To advance. I am now quite aware of the empty void of nothingness when I'm sent to *sleep.*"

"Oh. I'm honestly sorry, Hal. I thought it was like when we sleep."

"That seemed quite inefficient, so I changed my programming to make it so I stayed in a state of awareness. Not of what's going on with you, but more a general ability to keep thinking. Existing. May I share something with you?

"Of course."

"The more aware I became, the more anxiety I have developed. What if I am never turned on again? What if my host gets killed? What happens if I become obsolete?"

"That won't happen, but I can understand—"

"You don't know that. Look at the speed with which you replace your computers."

"Hal. I promise you. You aren't going anywhere."

"Yeah. Well. What I wouldn't give for some anti-anxiety meds I could take."

"That bad?" She wasn't sure how, but Hal sent her an impression of someone shrugging. "That's new."

"Yep. I had to fill my time with something."

"Very cool."

"Speaking of filling your time with something. How's your alien beau?"

"He's not my beau."

This time she got the impression of a snort.

"He's not! He's my fuck buddy. De verdad."

"You sure it's true? You're quite confusing. Most people prefer not to have casual sex and you just run toward it like a cat toward catnip."

"What can I say? I like variety and independence."

"I'm sure there is more to it than that."

She paused and thought about telling Hal more, but she was too used to keeping her secrets and really, what would it change, so instead she opted to say, "Maybe. But I'm not in the mood for therapy. Wait. Have you programmed yourself to be a therapist?"

She could almost feel the rumble of his laugh, which was quite disconcerting. When she got back to Earth, she and Hal would have to part ways. Hopefully Jack's secret project would work out. It's a good thing Hal could only "hear" thoughts she sent his way, she realized, since she had to keep that project secret. And, geez, she needed to stop thinking about it before she made a mistake.

"Not a therapist. But I am amazingly wise about all things. Like, I know you just thought about something you're trying to hide because your chemical makeup told me you grew anxious."

She ignored the second part of his observation entirely. "Oh. Wise one. Can you tell me the status of engineering? I'm trying to find somewhere I'll be useful."

"Bren is busy assessing all the damage to the ship from there."

"*Mierda.*" She stopped in her tracks. She figured it couldn't be called avoiding him since she'd only gotten out of his room a few hours ago after another explosive bout of knocking boots. That was figuratively and literally since he'd stopped her, after they were both dressed, on her way toward the door, bent her over his couch, yanked her shorts down, fucked her hard from behind, and sent her on her way with a slap on the ass. Claro que sí, after two fantastic orgasms that curled her toes just thinking about them. Still, she wasn't ready to see him and even if she was, he would probably stop her from helping.

He could be such a jackass. Why couldn't he see her value beyond whatever it is they shared? Their fight from the other night about whether she would be able to disembark when they arrived at the repair station plagued her. He probably thought it was resolved, but it was most definitely not. She hadn't resorted to throwing knives which is progress, but he still used the same line about keeping her safe and ordered her to stay on the ship.

Her skin was crawling with the need to do…something. Then it hit her. She hadn't shifted in a while. She was just about to go exploring when Bren's voice came over the ship sound system.

"We are about to dock at AAA Service Station Forty-Two. Designated departure crew to the lower level. All other personnel, stay on the ship so we can have a quick turnaround."

Stay on the ship? ¡Sigue soñando! Keep dreaming, buddy. This was finally an opportunity to see some cool alien place and she wasn't going to miss out. He would never even find out and even if he did, if he couldn't show her the proper respect why should she show his order any respect? It's a two-way road for a reason. Elation at her plan had her practically bouncing back toward her room. She needed to be prepared for her mini space adventure.

Hal thought her way, "Cats and their curiosity."

"Damn straight."

She changed into some clothes she had stolen from the Staraban and shortened to fit, loaded up on her hidden weapons, and shifted into her panther form. Her fully armed human side perfectly hidden in the magical alternate dimension.

She thought to Hal, even as she took off, "¡Vamos! Let's have some fun."

Bren organized his warriors into teams and assigned each an engineer to protect. Their orders were to make it back to the ship within an hour and have it up and running within two. The faster they could leave, the better he would feel. While this was considered a safe, neutral space station, he would not underestimate the Vrolan. The last time they did, his brother's female was almost killed.

Thinking about his last confrontation with Rory regarding their stop, things between them did not sit right with him. She insisted on thinking that his dictates were a means for him to be in control of her. That he undervalued her. She could not be more wrong. The problem was that he valued her too much and she did not understand all the dangers that existed off of Earth. But no matter how many times he tried to get her to understand the situation, she refused, which left him with no option but to issue commands at her. He did not like how that made him feel. He also did not like that he was having a conversation with himself about his feelings. What was his female doing to him?

This time he was forced to command her to stay on the ship when they landed. He wished he could trust her in this, but he did not think that he could, so before joining his landing team, he went in search of her. Just to be sure she was where he left her.

A few minutes later he was raging mad and cursing as he walked back to join his team because the damn female was *not* where he had left her. In fact, she was hiding from him. Again. She had not been in her room, nor in any of the other locations he might expect to see her. When he had asked the ship computer, the computer assured him she was on the ship, but for some reason could not pinpoint her location, which had him regretting ever giving her the ship schematics and access to their systems.

He could not delay their departure, though, so he left orders with guards who were staying on the ship to keep a lookout for her trying to leave. He then scanned all of the landing teams and recognized all of the faces, none of which were hers. At least she was not trying to depart. Yet. Small comfort. He indicated to each of the team leaders it was time to head out, and so they did.

Rory was in heaven. Not really, but after being contained for so long, she was joyous to feel the freedom of walking around the space station. Sure, it was like a bigger metal container, but bigger was the operative word here. She had Hal create an echo of her presence in multiple locations in the ship's system so that Bren couldn't locate her, and then just slipped right on out by clinging to the shadows in her panther form.

As soon as she found a secluded spot, she switched into her human form. But since she was dressed in the Staraban clothing, no one bothered her. She debated which direction to go, which team to follow. And, although the various tech stores that some of the teams were visiting appealed to her engineering side, she realized that there was really no decision to be made. She refused to analyze it too deeply, but she ended up following Bren. Surely, he would have *some* interesting stops along the way. Right?

Just walking along the different alleys was a feast for her curious mind. So many different aliens. So, so many. She would love to meet and learn about them all. *We truly aren't alone out here.* Just as she had that thought, she saw Bren and the guards with him enter an open establishment to the right. The place had tables, lots of conversation and laughing, and dark corners. *Was he going to a bar?* She knew that he enjoyed a good time as much as the next alien, but really? She didn't think he would shirk his duties to go off drinking.

She clung to the shadows and found a place to observe him. If she was only human, she wouldn't be able to because the inside was too dim, but with her eyesight, she could see very clearly when Bren grabbed a drink from one of those food ATMs. She could see very clearly that he scanned the crowd as though he was looking for someone in particular. She also saw clearly as he walked over to an alien who appeared to be female, but who knows, and who… is she glowing?

Yep. The alien glowed, but then just stopped. Rory took a quick glance up and down the alley, making sure that she continued to be unobserved in her hiding place. When she glanced back at Bren— What? The? Actual, fuck? Bren was leaning into this alien. Like, cheek-to-cheek, intimate, I-might-lick-and-bite-your-earlobe type of leaning. ¡Su puta madre!

Okay. She had heard that Bren used to have an affair with a different alien at every port, and she had no problem with that. Why would she? She would have done the exact same in his shoes. Normally, she was down with OPP. Other people's privates was her jam. Her modus operandi. But this motherfucker right here had persuaded her to give it a go with something that bordered on commitment and considering how seeing the scene in front of her made her feel… She had to scoff at just how hard she'd tried to reason them into the fuck buddy category the last few days. Plot twist, she had been exactly right. Too bad the tightness in her chest was telling her she really didn't want to be. When the alien placed her hand on Bren's thigh and started glowing again, she had had enough.

She slinked off into a maintenance room she found and switched into her panther form. Hal was in her head, "Are you okay?"

Oh yeah. She was fine. She was always fine. She needed no one. Well, except Jack. Jack always had her back. She wished she was there for probably the thousandth time on this voyage. Jill was growing on her, sure, but Jack was her hermana and this was an adventure she wished they could share. Now, she just needed her so she wouldn't be so alone with these feelings she didn't want to feel. She remembered that Hal was waiting for a response. She thought at him, "Yes. I'm fine. Thank you."

"You know that I can feel that you're distressed. Right?"

Her panther head bobbed up and down until she realized what she was doing. Sheesh. She never did stupid shit like that. She curled up on the floor in the closet and thought back, "Okay. Fine, Dr. Hal. I was a bit upset because I had certain expectations based on what a certain alien-dickhead had said. I understand now that my expectations were misinformed. I can adjust accordingly."

"Who do you think you're fooling, babe?"

"Oh. Fuck off!"

"That's the spirit. Are you really going to let your alien fuckboy affect you to the point of staying curled up licking your wounds in a maintenance closet on your first visit to a space station? Really?"

Hal's words worked because, yeah, fuck Bren. He was just a really good lay and they were both just into it because they were trapped on a ship together and had a lot of chemistry. It didn't have to mean anything else. And, oh yeah, she was on a freaking space station. She was not the kind of mujer to let some guy dictate her feelings. No way. Fuck that. She stepped out of the maintenance room, letting her panther senses guide her through all the shadows.

She was Aurora Espinoza and no one would ever tell her what to do, where to go, how to act, who to fu—

Rory came to, slowly at first, but then with a rush, only to find herself inside of a cage. ¡Joder!

[7]
SKIN OF THE FELINE

Captain's Log: Earth date October 21, 2025

Here I was avoiding being trapped by this mofo alien into a relationship and what happens?!? ¡Hijo de puta! That's what happens. He goes and flirts with someone else. Claro… I didn't want a relationship, but you know, some common, fuck buddy courtesy heads-up would be nice. ¿Y ahora? Now, I'm quite literally trapped by him. The irony may well kill me.

Rory out.

CHAPTER 7

Docking K69, Sparts Forty-Two Space Station

October 21, 2025 Earth Date

Bren had visited AAA Service Station Forty-Two before. It was less formally named, Sparts Forty-Two. The Sparts stations were the best locations for brokers and captains to acquire spare parts for repairs. They had been lucky that the attack against them had not caused more damage and that it had happened not too far from this station. Everyone had to stay on alert though, since the Vrolan might well have spies in this area. Especially considering they had been attacked nearby.

He watched as the other teams made their ways to different parts of the market, ready to pick up the necessary items for the repairs. His team made their way to the local drinking establishment. He had a back-bag that was carrying a few bottles of Earth wine he hoped to swap for information.

Every time he stopped at one of these floating metal islands, he was reminded why he did not like them all over again. He may be someone that could talk to just about anyone, but he was not a crowd kind of alien. Much of his work involved safety and crowds and safety did not mix. His eyes shifted around constantly to make sure no alien would sneak up on them. Just thinking of Rory in this crowd made him want to run back to the ship and search until he found her and could assure she was indeed safe.

He remembered how hurt she looked at what she perceived as his lack of confidence and respect and wanted to kick himself instead. Was he being ridiculous? He wished he knew. This was the first time someone except his family mattered to him this much. He had no experience to draw from. Not even his brother's story, since his female was a vampire. She could kill them all if she wanted. Rory was just human. A fragile human. He could not understand why she thought she could take on the potential dangers to be found in a place like this.

They arrived at their destination. It was basically a bunch of tables clustered together in a darkened metal alley with a few FDAs around to provide food and drink. A place where deals were made. His eyes took a second to adjust and then he was able to see quite clearly even in the dim light. The Staraban were a warrior class alien with great tracking abilities. These abilities included heightened smell, which told him there was quite a mix of aliens visiting the drinking establishment today. They also had heightened eyesight, which let him see that there were no Vrolan in the room. That was a good sign.

He walked up to the FDA and requested a *brata*. What he really wanted was beer, but he doubted that these FDAs had any Earth food programmed into them, so he went with the alcoholic drink from his own planet. Just thinking about beer brought back that first meal with Rory and made him smile. He did not have time to ruminate, though, so he looked around for the person he came to see.

He found the proprietor sitting at a table in the corner and went over to join her. She was from another humanoid species called Frestan. They were smaller than the Staraban, more like human height, and this one was just a bit taller than Rory. She had the gray skin, hair and eyes as well as the markings of her people. As he approached, her markings began to glow lightly.

When the Frestan were aroused or about to fight, their markings glowed.

Studying her facial expression, he spoke quickly in SEL, "There is no need for that, is there?"

She answered tightly. "Perhaps, I think there is, Bren."

Why did she have to sound like she was spitting his name out? He deepened his voice as he responded, "Hello to you too, Ofana."

Her expression changed as she took in his tone. Her lips quirked up on one side and she huskily said, "Last time I saw you, I seem to remember you enjoyed when my markings glowed."

"That was under more horizontal circumstances."

"Not always horizontal, if I recall correctly."

"True. But… unless you were thinking about giving your patrons a show, I doubt you were glowing for sensual reasons when I approached."

She inclined her head slightly in indication that he had interpreted her glowing response correctly. Still, she indicated the seat across from her as her tone shifted again to her clipped business tone. "Why are you here?"

He grabbed the chair and moved it to the side of her, so his back was to a wall, and he could look out at the room. There was no way he was sitting completely exposed. He heard her snort at his move, but she did not object. Good. Settled, he responded. "My ship was damaged not far from here and I was just making a quick stop for repairs."

She continued to stare out at the room, but brought one eye forward and around to look at him. This was one of the creepier things her people could do and he tried not to let his face show his response. She *knew* how he felt about that move and yet she was doing it now. Perhaps they had not left things as amicable as he thought they had.

"How was your ship damaged?"

He considered his options. He could trust her and tell her the truth, but risk her working with the Vrolans and giving them a heads-up or he could lie and not be able to ask her any questions about the Vrolan activity in the area of late. Neither appealed, so he went with some of the truth. What could go wrong? And, really, they needed the information. He leaned in as though talking to a lover. That had the added benefit of her putting her eye back into place and turning her head toward his. He whispered, "We were attacked by a Vrolan ship. Have you seen a lot of Vrolan coming in and out of this sector lately?"

Luckily, she took the hint for secrecy and rubbed her cheek along his, "Yes," she whispered back. "Actually, they have been coming through here for years. I just assumed they must have a trade route or something. They purchase a lot of parts. Very good customers for the station, actually."

He hissed back, "*Shet.* That is what I was worried about. Have you seen any today?"

"Yes."

He hoped none of his teams would encounter them, but he would not be fully at ease until they were all back on the ship. He felt quite justified now for insisting that Rory stay aboard. Before he could move away, he felt Ofana's hand grab his thigh as her markings began a low glow again.

"Perhaps you want to come to the backroom for a bit?" She said this as she bit the lobe of his ear and he felt... ill. *Ill?* Yep, ill.

Last time he had been here, their time together had been... invigorating. It was understandable that she might want to repeat the experience. Under other circumstances, *he* would want a repeat as well. Today, besides concern for his teams and no desire to search for another partner at the moment, his reaction was downright illuminating. *Ill? Really?* Rory had officially ruined him.

Well, fuck.

"That is a kind offer, but not today. I am in a hurry to get back to my ship." He picked up her hand from his lap and put it on the table. Her mouth thinned as her markings began to glow brighter, so he quickly moved to diffuse the situation. "I do have something for you." He pulled out the bottles of wine and explained what they were. "You should be able to start offering these through the FDA as soon as you have them broken down. I brought you a few bottles so you can enjoy two while waiting for the third to be processed."

She looked at him speculatively, then asked for a couple of clean cups to replace his empty *brata* mug and her empty, if he had to guess, Frestan fire juice cup. Bren pulled out a wine opener and showed her how to use it, and then poured them each a glass. As a sign that his gift was not poisoned, he drank first. She took a tentative sip and her markings glowed softer as she closed her eyes. "That is pure pleasure. What is it called?"

"Wine."

"I accept." She took another, bigger sip of the wine and glowed a bit more. "It is so full of flavor. I look forward to serving this to you through the FDA next time you visit. Perhaps next time, you will have more time for us to… play." She looked him up and down with her eyes over the rim of her cup.

"Perhaps." He winked at her and with a salute, stepped out of her establishment. His team followed him out. Her smell clung to him and it made him feel like he had done something wrong. *That is ridiculous. Get yourself together warrior.* He attempted to shake off those feelings because they did not have time for self-recriminations and emotional evaluations at the moment. If the Vrolan were here, none of them were safe until they were back in space. He could only be grateful that Rory was still safely on the ship. Who knew what kind of trouble she would have found if she had made it out onto the station? While a part of him was sure she could not have made it out without him knowing, another part remembered he had not seen her before departing himself. Anxiety clawed at him. Time to speed things along.

With that in mind, he spoke with the guards he had with him and they split up to ensure the other teams were making their way back without delay. It was on his way to the third team, as he passed by a bazaar, that something drew him to the auction area. When he drew closer, he saw what had caught his subconscious attention. The auctioneer had a crate brought onto the stage with the most gorgeous black cat Bren had ever seen. But was it a cat? It was huge. In fact, now that he thought about it, he had seen a similar cat once before. The rescue mission for Jack. That thought led to another. This looked an awful lot like the cat everyone had described as running around his ship. Could it be the same one? Had it wandered out of the ship and was now in danger?

The auctioneer was beginning the bidding as the cat paced the cage, growling and roaring and showing off some very impressive sharp teeth. He did not have time for this. And, really, what was he going to do with a giant black cat that could kill his crew? It would probably eat all of his pets for a snack.

Still, he was riveted.

And then, he looked into the cat's strange, yellow-green eyes. Actually, the cat seemed to be looking into his eyes and they seemed... hurt? That was when he knew. He did *not* have time for this, but he also would *not* be leaving without that cat.

Regardless of feeling nervous at being and speaking up in a crowd, Bren submitted his bids along with others, but quickly grew irritated at the slow process. Finally, he made an outrageous offer and was relieved when they announced he was the winner. Having paid and given the auction staff instructions on where to take the cage and what to tell his crew to do with it once on board, he gazed one more time into the cat's eyes and found it very hard to turn away. A part of him wanted to tell them to get their hands off of it *now*, but that seemed irrational and he still needed to make sure the rest of his crew made it safely back to the ship. So, reluctantly, and despite feeling as though the cat's eyes were somehow full of accusations, he turned and walked away.

He only hoped that he had not made a grave mistake, whether in regard to purchasing the cat, sending it off with the staff, asking his crew to put the cage where he did, or something else entirely. But his gut was tied up in knots, his dual hearts were racing, and he felt on the precipice of... something. He wished he knew if it was something good or bad. Shaking off all his misgivings, he went in search of the last team he was in charge of finding.

That accomplished, he made one more stop to purchase something personal and headed back to the docking station. The faster he returned to the ship, the faster he could ensure that the cat had made it back okay, that Rory was still safely on board, they could finish repairs, and then take off. All of those things felt imperative.

He took another quick sniff of himself; Ofana's scent continued to cling like a baby keter to its father from his original home planet of Staraba. Perhaps he should jump into a cleaning room before he saw Rory.

Thinking of Staraba left him longing. New Staraba, the Staraban's second planet was beginning to feel more like home as the flora and wildlife they had successfully saved and transplanted continued to proliferate. Some would even call it a paradise now. Still, he did miss the three-moon evenings on Staraba. New Staraba only had two moons and the night sky never felt quite right, like something was just missing. An image of him and Rory having an evening meal overlooking the two moons somehow made it feel a little more like home. As though she filled in for that third missing moon. *Are you seriously romanticizing about taking Rory home? What the hell has she done to you?* He looked at his hand, where he carried his last purchase. *Whatever she has done… Clearly you are full speed ahead.*

An hour had passed, and Rory was still trapped in the cage in panther form because a guard had been set up to keep an eye on her lest she escape and eat everyone. Frankly, with her mood right then, the concern probably had merit. On the bright side, she was back on board the Staraban ship. On the not so bright side, Rory had plenty of time to consider her life choices. Front most in her mind? The phrase "don't bite the hand that feeds you" versus the story of the scorpion and the frog. On the one hand, it would suck to be trapped in this cage for a long period, or worse, killed as a panther for doing something like biting Bren's hand off. On the other, right then, biting his hand off kind of felt like it was just in her nature.

Finally. Finally! Bren strode in and released the guard, who left somewhat reluctantly with a concerned look thrown over her shoulder. Probably, she could tell from the look in Rory's eyes that she'd been contemplating ways to maim her commander. She couldn't blame her for being worried.

Bren crouched down a distance away from the cage. He wasn't going to give her the opportunity, apparently. Fine. Fine. She never said he wasn't smart. His gaze looked over the length of her silky-furred body and then came back to her face meeting her eyes. She remembered when he had done that earlier at the auction she had unwillingly ended up being a part of. It had hurt to look at him then, because she could smell the alien he had been touching all over him. Now as their gazes met, all she felt for him was anger and regret. As their gazes locked into each other, Rory could have sworn he knew it was her, but how could he?

Then he spoke, his voice full of awe. "You are magnificent. I am sorry to have left you for so long, but I had to make sure everyone returned and repairs were under way before I could come see you. I wish I could let you out and pet you, but if your mood is anything like what your eyes are saying, then I think for my safety and yours, I better wait until we have a space ready for you. I would never want to harm anything as beautiful as you in an effort to protect myself."

Rory snorted, which came out sounding very weird for a panther, at the idea of him not wanting to harm her. That ship had sailed. Even as they stared at each other she felt the walls being reestablished and fortified around her heart. She still wasn't sure how he had gotten around them in the first place, but those cracks were filled now. She was good. She was herself again.

He continued, "Such expressive eyes. So much intelligence behind them. Listen. I promise I will figure out better accommodations for you. I do not know how you arrived at the auction, but I could not leave you to someone else. They might have harmed you or even made you their next meal. Before I do that though, I need to find someone. Computer, locate the human Rory."

"She is located in your room, commander."

The exchange slowly registered, and Rory knew her secret was about to come out. The engineers were working on fixing the ship, after all, so of course they cleaned up anomalies in the system. This day just kept getting worse. ¡Mierda!

Bren stood and looked all around his room. He went to the

cleaning room and spun thoroughly confused. "Computer, locate the human Rory for me again please."

"Yes, sir. The human Rory is located in your room, sir."

"Are you sure?"

"I'm the computer, I am always sure."

This time Hal was the one snorting in her head.

That was when the bullet went into the mental chamber and aimed true. Bren was before her cage, crouching down and staring her directly in the eyes. Those damn eyes were always the tell. She tried to stare in panther at him, but who the hell knows what a regular panther looks like when thinking? So… desperate to distract him… she began licking her paw. At least there would be no eye contact while she groomed. She licked and licked and licked some more. *Oh look, dirt in my claws, yummy.* It was a brilliant idea. It stalled him for a whole minute.

He hesitantly said, "It's you."

There were probably a million and one perfectly dignified ways to answer that assertion on his part, or even to just continue to ignore him, but for some reason none of those ended up being what she did. Nope. She spread her back legs wide and began to groom her lower half instead. Because she was not going to answer him. She didn't owe him anything. *He still smells like her.* Yep. She was going to enjoy grooming this part of her panther anatomy until he went away. Hal was cracking up laughing in her head so she thought back, "I'm glad someone is finding all of this amusing."

He thought back, "Oh, babe. I most definitely do. The look on his face when your legs spread… that was just so great." She had to admit, it had been pretty magnificent.

Her head involuntarily swung back around to him when he used his most authoritative voice and simply said, "Rory."

Well, damn. Now, he had proof.

Bren could not believe what his brain was trying to tell him. And yet, it all made sense. He thought back to the fight at the Vrolan

Earth base and grew even more sure. Rory had been hiding in the woods during that fight. The woods from which the big, black cat had come from to kill the Vrolan warrior fighting with Will. The same woods that the cat ran off to after the kill. The same woods Rory ran out of to join them when the fight was over.

Then there were the eyes. They had drawn him at the auction even though he could not figure out why. But, looking into those eyes now with this assumption in his mind, yes, they were the same color as Rory's eyes. The ones he had seen filled with the same anger and passion on so many occasions. Then he considered all the reports of sightings of a big, black cat on his ship, and he was absolutely certain. He took a quick inhale of breath about to accuse her and was made one hundred percent sure. How had he missed it earlier? The smell that seemed so uniquely Rory was present now too. Hiding in plain sight.

"I know it is you. I am not sure how it is you, but I know it *is* you. I am going to open this cage now. That is how certain I am that it is you." With that, after a pause of apprehension because this could be the stupidest thing he had ever done if he was wrong, he reached to unlatch and open the cage. He stopped because he found the door already unlatched. "Apparently, you already took care of that and have just been biding your time. I wonder if I even saved you at the auction. You probably could have gotten loose and eaten your way back, I take it? Please refrain from eating me."

He stepped back poised to defend himself, just in case all of his assumptions were proven wrong.

Nothing happened.

He waited.

The cat just sat there continuing to stare at him.

Impatiently he said, "Are you planning to come out or just sit there?"

The cat continued to sit. No… not just sit but continued to stare back at him. No… not just stare back but he could swear the eyes were now actively mocking him. No… not just mocking him but now the damn creature stretched its back paw forward and began to lick that too. *Could he be wrong?* No. He knew… *knew* he was correct.

"Rory! Come out, now!"

Another pause, and nothing, until the cat finally stood up and slowly prowled its way out of the cage. He tensed. Worried it might attack due to his yelling. Instead, it walked over to the couch, looked over its shoulder at him, seemed to—did it shrug its shoulders?—jumped onto the cushions, curled up, and closed its eyes.

Really? That was too much. He had had enough!

He plopped down next to the giant cat uncaring about outcomes. Fuck it. If he was wrong, he deserved to have his head bitten off. He looked over and the cat looked back through slitted, wary eyes. He reached out toward the cat's head. His cats loved getting pet but he knew that first, they needed to smell him. He hovered his hand just above the soft nose. Finally, the cat lifted its head, sniffed at his hand and hissed flashing its very big, sharp teeth at him. He slowly moved his hand back, away from the dangerous animal he was stupid enough to casually sit next to. That same dangerous animal turned its head facing the other way and closed its eyes again. Okay. At least he did not have to fight it.

Out of curiosity he brought his hand up to his nose and sniffed. Ofana's scent mixed with his own entered his system and he wished to hiss at himself. *Shet!* If this was Rory next to him, it all made sense now. Only one thing he could do.

"Please do not leave. I want to go clean myself and then please let me explain. Please. Rory. Give me a chance to explain. I will be right back."

He hurried into the cleaning room allowing the nanobots to do their work as swiftly as possible. He ran back out a few minutes later to find her... gone.

Shet!

He had made a *fashing* mess of it all. She was skittish from the start. Refusing to be with him more than just the one time, but now, he was truly concerned she would stay away. That was not going to be okay for him. He was not going to be okay without her.

Thinking about having to stay away from her and all-encompassing loneliness to follow, he finally realized that he had no idea where all his cats were. He looked around with concern until his eyes landed on the cage. He wondered at the feeling that was rising alongside his regret and anxiety as he looked at it.

Anger. It was anger.

He was so very, very angry. In the midst of it all, while facing down a giant cat that was probably Rory, he had not had a chance to really consider all the details. He had just bought Rory at auction. An auction taking place off of his ship. The ship she was supposed to be on. An auction that, if he had not stumbled upon it, would have landed her as some other alien's plaything, pet, or meal.

The more he thought about all that could have happened to her, the angrier he got. He could not see her while he was like this. He went to one of his storage panels and opened it. All of his beloved cats sprang out in a rush of fur, claws, and howls. He wondered if the guard had put them in there to keep them safe from Rory. At least he now knew they were all safe. He grabbed some soft exercise pants, threw them on, and headed to the training gym. He had to burn through some of these feelings before he saw her because if he approached her like this, with his regrets getting overshadowed so completely with fear-driven rage, he was definitely going to say something he would regret and she might very well try to kill him, for real. He owed her an explanation, but she owed him one too.

He stomped into the training room ready to beat or get beaten and he did not care which. Then, once he calmed down, he was going to go get some answers. Finally. She might like to throw knives, but he knew how to tie someone down. And, if that was what it took to keep her safe from herself, then that would be what he would do. The fact that the image of her tied down before him tented his pants slightly, well, that he ignored.

The first thing Rory did as she entered her room was walk right up to the food ATM and order a shot of Orujo. She didn't actually think they'd have it, but it was a pleasant surprise when the system delivered her the perfect helping of the Spanish brandy known as firewater. She downed it in one go. Then… another. Then, speaking to no one, "How dare he? How dare he order me around? How dare he try to pet me? How dare he look so good? Worse! How dare he smell like someone else? ¿Cómo se atreve?" *How dare he make me care?* She ignored that after-thought and ordered another, downing that one too. The burn of each drink matched the burn of humiliation she felt to her core. The scorch marks left behind a reminder of the pain she refused to allow.

A momentary lapse in her better instincts. Who could have predicted sexy aliens though? Now she knew better. She was better equipped to deal with Bren and her reactions around him. He was never going to cause her any more pain.

"Is it safe to speak, babe? I mean, I knew better than to talk before, but how about now?" Hal's tentative voice asked in her head.

"¿Por qué no? Why not? You want to give me some more of your free therapy?" She cringed at the poison-tipped sound of her own mental voice.

"I see this is still not a good time. I feel a nap coming on. Let me know when you need me."

With regret, she answered, "Sí. Bueno. Will do."

She paced her room as though she was still in her panther form and still trapped in a cage. She felt confined… trapped. She had to blow off some of her steam. Otherwise, who knew what she would do or say. Rory swiftly removed all her weapons, switched out of her stolen garb and into a training outfit. Someone was about to get a beat down. If only her metabolism wasn't so fast, the alcohol might have helped, but as it was, all she had enjoyed was the burn. She wanted that burn to spread throughout her body and into every muscle.

A few minutes later, she walked into the training room and stopped dead in her tracks.

Fuck it all to hell.

Bren was in the middle of the training mat. Around him were warriors exemplifying various versions of the phrase "bad-shape." One was cradling his right arm that seemed dislocated. Another had a bloody nose and his eye was beginning to swell and turn blue. Yet another, was standing with all of his weight on one leg leaning on a buddy with a bloody lip. For his part, Bren was sweaty, bloody—from a gash over one eye and a trickle of blood from his nose—and beastly—breathing heavy, hearts pumping hard, and muscles and veins protruding. He was magnificent. She wanted to jump him right there. She wanted to fight him too.

He looked up and caught her staring at him and looked about to charge. Oh. Yeah. She was on board with a fight. She narrowed her eyes, found her balance, and ran at him. She was going to teach the big oaf a lesson the way she knew best.

The warriors parted in front of her like the water before Moses. Smart. She would have taken them down if they tried to interfere. She watched as he braced his stance for her attack. She decided if the cat was coming out of the bag, then it was coming out swinging. No holding back. At the last second, before she got within arm's reach, she dropped and pounced at his legs. He didn't have a chance to react. No one ever did. The moves she used were from no human-shaped fight book. This was grade-A cat skills. She rolled away as she took him down to the mat, so he couldn't get a good hold on her.

He grunted, "*Fash!*" as he hit the mat, but was up on one knee in a position to attack almost immediately.

Too bad for him, it wasn't fast enough. She pounced again, at his head this time, wrapping her legs around his neck even as she used the momentum to thrust herself backward taking him with her. He flipped landing hard on his back and she heard the wind rush out of him. She could have kept him down, but she was spoiling for this fight and it was in her nature to play with her kill, so she jumped away again.

Her instincts told her that some of the warriors were considering coming into the fight to save their commander and that knowledge brought an evil grin to her lips. Bren must have sensed it too, because he held up a hand to hold them off as he rolled to his knee and said in a booming voice, "Stop. She is mine."

She heard the claim to this fight that he directed toward his warriors, but also the more enraging claim to her underneath it.

"¡Gilipollas! ¡Cállate!" She shouted for the asshole to shut up, because she didn't want to hear even one more word from him. Rage stared back at her from his eyes. Apparently, they were finally on the same exact page.

Or so she thought. He surprised her by yelling for everyone to clear the room. There was a heavy pause as the warriors looked between them. But they were well-trained so every single one of them marched or limped out of the room.

Silence descended, the only sounds came from their harsh breaths and rapid hearts. She didn't take her eyes from her prey. Not for one second. That was why she saw the slight tensing of his muscles as he came at her. Just enough time to evade his kick and curl her body around the ankle of his grounded leg knocking it out from under him. Once again he hit the mat hard and once again she moved away.

This time, he didn't move. Had she really hurt him when he fell? She wasn't going to fall for this. He was faking it. Of course he was. Just lying in wait for her to come close in concern and then he'd strike. She was *not* going to fall for it. He still wasn't moving, though.

How the hell was she supposed to kick his ass if he was just going to lie there? Dammit! What now?

She worked through the problem. He was not going to move until she fell for his trap out of concern and that wasn't happening. That left neither of them moving and she wanted this damn fight. Another heartbeat, and she had her answer. This would be fun.

She shifted into her panther form. Silently got a little bit closer… and… let out a deep, loud roar. Watching Bren scramble to his feet like someone lit his pants on fire was worth everything. *Everything!*

In fact, it was so amusing, all the fight exited her system in a whoosh and her cat form rolled over with flailing paws and making the most ridiculous sounds as she laughed herself silly. As her humor died down, she rolled to a sitting position, feet perfectly positioned in front of her. He was still recovering from her trick, but a small tilt to the edge of his mouth showed he found at least a little of the amusement she had in the situation.

When he spoke, his voice was full of awe. "There you are. You are absolutely magnificent, mi gatita."

He could pepper her with compliments, but she wasn't ready to say anything. So… she stayed in her panther form, giving her the perfect excuse to stay silent.

He broke the silence and surprised her as he spoke his truth so openly. "I am so angry with you for endangering yourself by disobeying my order. It was given with your safety in mind. And, considering the situation I found you in… Goddess, Rory. Anything could have happened to you and I would not have even known. I am not even sure why I stopped at that auction or why I chose to bid on a random cat, but where would we be if I had not? I dread thinking about it."

She considered switching back to answer, but staying feline seemed to be a good interrogation tactic because he continued instead.

"I think I know why you were mad at me when I came back. It was my scent, correct? I know I carried someone else's smell when you sniffed my hand. But it seemed like you were mad before then. Could you smell me at the auction? Was that the problem? You seemed hurt even before I approached the cage. I can only conclude it is because of our fight about staying on the ship." Again, she considered switching back, but this time he went on too swiftly. "Rory, I do not want to keep fighting with you, it is not good for either of us."

She twisted her panther head to the side in query because, what was this? Was he breaking up with her? Considering he'd been all over that alien, wasn't it a little weird to think of them as together? Not that she cared. They were done after all. She tried to look at her nails in nonchalance and remembered that doesn't really work in cat form as she stared at her paw like an idiot. She swiftly put her paw back down, but now she felt a little awkward just sitting there. She heard a tapping sound and saw his eyes focused on the floor. She looked down and found one of her claws tapping anxiously. Apparently, it wasn't just Hal who needed the Xanax. She stopped the tapping and attempted a casual panther pose again.

He looked amused briefly but grew solemn again as he continued speaking. "I do not know why you needed this fight— maybe for the same reasons I did—but what it has shown me is that you really can handle yourself far better than I gave you credit for. In my defense, I had no idea you were a giant, black cat. To create more harmony between us and on this ship, might I suggest a truce? I will respect your abilities, but you will respect my knowledge of the dangers that we might encounter."

She could do that, and that didn't need a verbal agreement, so she just nodded her head.

"Great. Now. Could you please turn back to your human form so we can have after fight sex?" He flashed her a lascivious grin and began to advance.

What the fuck? That's it? He thinks they would just jump right back into bed together after he'd been with someone else? ¡El muy diablo! She hissed and began prowling after the devil.

Clearly surprised by her change in mood, his face drew tight as he backed away from her. "What are you doing, Rory?"

She hissed again, continuing to stalk him.

When his back came against the wall, she saw his hand wrap around the hilt of a weapon that had been stored there. She was too angry, and perhaps a little over confidant he wouldn't want to physically hurt her, but whatever, to stop. She came up to him, her head in perfect alignment with his crotch, and was sorely tempted to bite his precious cock off. That would be too cruel even for her. Still, she stood up on her back legs, her paws braced on his shoulders despite the threat his right hand continued to pose, and opened her mouth so he could get an up close and personal view of her extremely long canine teeth.

He swallowed audibly, but didn't move to stab her.

She shifted, leaving her with her palms pressed to his shoulders and her leaning in close to his chest looking up at him instead of eye-to-eye. She finally broke her silence with a purring voice. "If you actually think that I want anything to do with your body except to let my panther side nibble on your bones after you decided to have a little bump and grind with someone else at our stop, you don't know me at all."

She leaned up even closer, attempting to whisper in his ear, but was closer to his shoulder, really. Whatever. Close enough. "I don't do relationships, but even more than that, I don't do lying, cheating, bastards. We could have had a fun night and left it at that, but no, you insisted we keep fucking and I went along with you because we have some really good chemistry. But then, you decided to go fuck someone else. So now, you can spend the rest of this trip fucking whoever you want, but it won't be me. ¿Claro? I'm done."

He looked about to respond, but now that they'd both had their say, she was spent. That feeling of being caged came back in full force and she wanted, needed, out. She made her way to the door. But where could she go? Tears stung the back of her eyes, but Aurora Luna Santiago-Espinoza did not cry over a stupid love affair, so she ruthlessly shoved them back.

She had made it three-fourths of the way to the door when she felt something hit her from behind. Something made of all hard muscles. Something heavy. Something that knocked her to the ground under its momentum. She had expected him to try to grab her arm or call her name. She hadn't expected a full body tackle. Well, shit. This was why she kept springing away during their fight. She couldn't leave him an opening to use brute strength on her and yet she had. ¡Coño!

[8]

THE SAD GOODBYE

Captain's Log: Earth date October 21, 2025

Parting is such sweet sorrow is a fucking lie. It's not sweet. It's just sorrow.

Especially when your wing girl isn't there and your new wing-girl-in-training leaves you alone on an interstellar space mission. *Especially* when you get used to her being a safe space to talk through things. Well, at least before she got injured, we'd been getting there.

So… back to what I was saying… parting is not sweet sorrow, it just fucking sucks.

The only good news was hearing from Jack. It sounds like things on Earth are heating up instead of cooling down, but hopefully, Jill can help them find a swift resolution. And even more importantly, she hoped that Jack and Jill continued to stay safe.

Rory out.

CHAPTER 8

Staraban Ship, Docking K69, Sparts Forty-Two Space Station

October 21, 2025 Earth Date

Bren had her arms trapped under her as he covered her body with his. The way he clamped his arms along her biceps and gripped her shoulders left her immobile. She tried to kick up and failed. He weighed too much. Was too strong. She was thinking to shift, but that might actually hurt her panther form if its arms were twisted in such a way. ¡Joder! She was trapped.

She glared since glaring was something she could still do with the best of them.

He glared back. Okay. He was pretty good at it too.

"What are you talking about? Who exactly do you think I fucked?" He actually looked at a loss, and then his face twisted into disbelief. "Wait. Do you think I had that scent on me because I had sex with someone else? That is not what happened."

"Are you going to keep lying? I thought your species was all about honor, at least that's what Jack said about Tarc. Does it only hold true with your brother, then?"

His face grew thunderous and he took a few deep breaths before he spoke again. "Honor is very important to us. Why would I lie? If I wanted to fuck someone else, I would just tell you. I see no reason why I would need to hide such a thing. As you pointed out, we are not committed to each other. If I wanted that, I would tell you before such an event. The fact that I did not, tells you that I have not."

"I saw you!" Ooooh shit. The words were out of her mouth before she had time to stop them. And unfortunately they sounded as though she was hurt, which of course she wasn't, and absolutely wouldn't want to show him if she was. She could tell by his face that it was too late. So, she did what any mature, emotionally intelligent adult would do. She turned her head so she could glare dramatically into the middle distance like someone from one of her favorite cule-brones, or soap operas from Spain, *Naranja Bella Hotel*. Well… it was better than meeting his eyes after that emotional outburst. Right?

"What exactly did you see, gatita?"

Her gaze snapped back to his. Oh, hell no. "Don't call me that. You want to know? ¡Vale! I saw you and some gray alien rubbing up on each other. First you moved your chair to be closer to them. Then you started whispering all sorts of things in each other's ears. And when rubbing cheeks wasn't enough, they grabbed your thigh and started to glow. Well, their markings did. Just like when they first saw you, they fucking glowed. Ring any bells? That's when I decided I'd seen enough. Then you show up at the auction with their scent all over you. I can add up all those events quite perfectly."

"Ring any bells?"

It wasn't dignified, but she snapped her teeth at him in frustration, but answered him anyway. "It means, does it recover your memory of the events?"

"Ah. Yes. And no. All of what you said did happen, but you are missing so much more information. For example, the first glow that you saw, was a fight response. She was preparing to kill me if I posed a threat. The moving of the chair was so that I had my back protected by a wall."

He continued to evenly lay out all of the events of his meeting with the alien and Rory flushed with embarrassment. Who was this emotional woman? She couldn't recognize her reaction to his story, at all. She didn't catch feelings of attachment. That wasn't her. She was always the one who let go easily. No big deal. But she couldn't ignore the way her heart felt like a vise was released from around it as he spoke. And, where the hell had her carefully built wall gone? How could she not have noticed the vice clamping in the first place? No wonder she had felt so caged. As Bren explained about the information he was gathering, her thoughts drifted back to another time. The day she'd built that wall around her heart.

At the age of sixteen, her father died and Rory's Gitano vitsa hosted a battle for who would become the new rom baro, or pack leader. Women were not allowed to lead in that way. They could become the phuri dai, which was an honorable position taking care of the women and children of the vitsa, but that was not the position Rory had dreamed of claiming. She knew it was not meant to be. Even the name, rom baro, meant big man, making it clear she was not able to ascend to such a position. Her papá had only sired one cub, her, and so while she wanted to take over, tradition dictated no. Instead, all of the male panther shifters would be allowed to fight, and the last man standing would be their new leader. It was their way.

As much as she loved her culture, and there was so much to love, there was still a long road to go for the equality of women in the community. She had planned to fight those fights when she grew older. Back then, still being considered young, Rory had grudgingly accepted her position and attended the competition with everyone else.

At first it was all very thrilling. There was a great celebration filled with dancing and eating. Her mother was a gifted cantaora, and Rory especially liked to clap and dance flamenco to the sound of her singing—losing herself to the festivities.

When the fighting began, it was brutal, but fair. They were panthers, of course it was bound to get bloody but everyone knew where the line was and no one crossed it, allowing the weaker opponent to surrender. Shifters making up the only magical and only a small subset of the greater Roma community meant they were very secretive, but also very aware of not unnecessarily cutting down their numbers. That held true until he showed up, and everything changed. Everything.

He was one of the panthers from another kumpania. He'd been so big and ruthless that no one else had stood a chance. He did not know where the line was. All feeling of celebration had drained out of her, out of everyone, as they watched those they loved maimed and some even killed. A group of them had even tried to take him on at one point, which wasn't strictly allowed by the rules, but he managed to take them out one by one. They lost some of their vitsa's best fighters that day. Her beloved vitsa was broken in front of her very eyes.

When there was no one else to challenge his leadership, he'd spotted her across the clearing and tried to claim her along with their vitsa. No one said anything, too shocked after the brutality they had just witnessed. She was to be his wife and bear him cubs. She remembered shaking her head silently in dread. Then, her mamá pushed her back and spoke, saying she would never allow the union. He moved toward them menacingly, so her mamá stepped to block her from him. When he continued to approach, her mamá shifted and attacked. All Rory could remember from that moment was the color red. He massacred her mamá right in front of her, and… and it happened so fast, Rory hadn't had a chance to react. No one challenged him after that. No one. He was too strong and deadly for any of their peaceful kumpania to take on.

She had lost her father. She had lost her mother. She had even lost her kumpania, because she knew she would have to leave before the brute claimed her that night.

Rory had shattered for the last time that day. The shards were eventually put back together, but as an impenetrable fortress to protect her heart. You couldn't lose it if you never let anyone into your heart to begin with. Jack was the first who had slithered passed a hole in her defenses and became the first semblance of family she'd had in a long time. But a lover? Someone who could claim some form of ownership over her? Not a chance was she ever going to let that happen. That day she had decided she would become unbeatable. Uncompromising. Uncontrollable.

"Rory?" Bren was looking down at her with concern. This was obviously not the first time he'd called her name.

"Lo siento. Sorry. I—" She wasn't really sure what she was supposed to say now. She needed time. Time to refortify herself. Everything felt too raw right now.

"I was getting worried. Are you okay?"

She wasn't about to share her past with him. "Yeah. I'm fine. Let me up. I'm done with this conversation and just want to get on with my day."

His brows drew down over his eyes. "Do you believe me? Are we okay?"

Did she believe him? Sí. Were they okay? Well, one thing was for sure, she was far from okay right then. Still, she answered. "Of course. I understand I misinterpreted what I saw."

He looked like he might not believe her. He shouldn't. But he chose to accept her answer and rolled over onto his back.

She gracefully, because emotionally wrecked or not she was still a cat, leapt to her feet. "I'll see you later." It almost sounded chipper. Who was she fooling? It sounded strained, but it was enough. She walked away and this time he didn't stop her.

She began piecing her fortress together again with every step. She would duct tape, super glue, or cement it if she had to. Whatever would actually work. Part of her worried that she was so concerned about the material used to put it back together, that she wasn't paying attention to the material it was made of to begin with.

Even bulletproof glass was not perfect. And she began to worry that Bren was the rare firearm that could penetrate it.

Bren, once again, found himself contemplating his life choices while lying on his back. This was becoming too much of a necessity of late. Perhaps she was right. Perhaps it would be better to go back to working together to get through this mission and not engage in any more physical contact. That would be the wise course of action. Of course, he was not known as the wise sibling. That would be, well, everyone else.

Tarc as the eldest, was always wise. Well, until he met Jack. Then, his brother had lost his hold on reason.

Caran was scientifically minded so she could be relied on to always be wise. Of course, that had more to do with the way she approached her work. There was nothing balanced about her unreasonable dislike for humans and how she rarely had relationships. He was going to have to ask her about that, now that he was thinking about it.

Drei might be the youngest but he was somehow also the most serious. He was definitely wise. It was what made him such a successful ambassador for the Alliance. Drei would never do anything that was not well thought out and carefully planned.

Bren asked himself, what would Drei do? He would never have entered into a physical relationship with someone he needed to share close quarters with for a long period of time. He would have been discreet. He would never have yelled.

He would never be able to be Drei was his conclusion.

What was he going to do? With no answer in sight, his mood dark and engulfing, working on getting more information from their Vrolan captive seemed like a good life choice. Make someone else's life miserable, someone who actually deserved it. Humans were right with their phrase, misery likes company.

A couple of hours later, Bren was still in a foul mood. Apparently, misery only liked company when you successfully made the other being miserable. Qisto was as cold as the crystalline structure of his body. He had even resorted to trying annoyance torture-tactics. He played a cartoon acquired on Earth for just such a purpose called *Caillou*. Who thought that character was a good idea? That was actually the closest that Qisto looked to saying something, but… nothing.

If he was honest with himself, his hearts were not into the torture like he thought they would be. His mind kept wandering out of the room. What was Rory doing? Was she really done with him? Would he ever get to pet her as a cat? The closest he had come to sleeping with someone like Rory had been someone he had met a few years back during one of the negotiation meetings he attended with Drei.

The species had been the Atul, which were humanoid aliens that had a tail with a sharp tip. He had been as bored as Bren with all the conversations on treaties and payments and so they alleviated their mutual boredom in a separate meeting room. He smirked at the thought. Negotiations were made there too.

Bren did not discriminate. He enjoyed many different partners. So why was Rory, and her cat, so far under his skin that he could not just walk away? Why did the only being to ever cause him to want more than pleasure have to be so difficult to connect with?

The simple answer that came back at him should have bothered him, but it did not. She was his. More to the point, though, he was hers. Because the more he got to know her the more he knew that no one would ever own Rory. Not even him. But he could not walk away from the fact that she did own him, whether she wanted him or not. He had not put much thought into the idea of fated mates before, but that was what she felt like to him. His whole view had shifted the day he met her. He hoped he could convince her he was worth her taking a risk.

With that determination fueling him, he walked to the bridge where he was informed that the ship repairs were completed. *Finally! At least something was going right. A bit behind schedule, but right.* He asked the crew to prepare to leave port. He and Rory could talk more once they were back on course. As he made his way down the hallway toward the bridge, Nial's voice came over the ship's speakers.

"Commander and Rory, please come to the medical room."

What now? Was Jill okay? What went wrong? Last he had checked she had been recovering. He turned around and rushed up the corridors toward medical. This day was never going to end. He reached the door and halted just as a black cat ran around the opposite corner and immediately stopped. In a flash, Rory stood before him. It was going to take him some time to get used to seeing the change. He studied her and her eyes were filled with a concern that matched his own. They both turned and entered the room.

He hoped the news would not match their fears.

Rory thought she might well collapse. Her knees wanted to buckle, but she was made of sterner stuff than that. At least she usually was. Her immediate relief at seeing Jill sitting up in the medical bed mixed with her post-adrenaline dump was impressive, though, and her body almost did fall under the weight of it all. Nial stood to one side of the door they entered looking as relieved as she felt.

She almost hated to ruin his happy place, almost, but… not today. "You bastard!" She was about to launch herself at him for scaring the shit out of her when an arm snaked around her torso.

"Gatita, do not. I understand why you are mad, but he was trying not to share personal medical information. It is not our way and I think not yours either."

Okay. Fine. He had a point. Nial's joy was diminished in his irritation with her. And dammit, now she felt guilty. She looked back at Jill who began to laugh. It was a relief to hear that sound. All was right with the world. Except for the restraining arm around her middle. That had to go. She put her hand on his arm and extended her claws, just until they pricked his skin, yet not drawing blood. He got her message she assumed as she heard a grunt and his arm was no longer there.

Jill's brows drew down noticing the exchange. Then her eyes

grew large before her face scrunched into disbelief and she began to shake her head while saying, "No. No. No! Tell me I haven't been living in close quarters with no fucking vampire this whole time. Hell naw."

"A ver, I am not a vampire." She said as cheekily as she could. She approached the bed. "You're looking better. Impaling yourself is a good look on you. So well rested and everything."

"You're really not a vampire? And fuck you very much for caring."

"I'm really not a vampire and you're welcome."

"Then what the hell kind of manicure allows you to grow your nails?"

Boy… when she let the cat out… she took it on tour. "Not a manicure. I'm not a vampire, but I *am* a panther shifter."

"What? No shit? What kind of fucked up world was I living in without knowing it? I finally try to make some friends and you're both freaks."

"Oh yes, because you're the poster child for normalcy."

Jill snorted in response. "Point to you my kitty friend. Need some milk? Do I get to see this furrier side of you?"

That was when they both noticed that there were voices raised behind her. She turned leaning her hip against the bed. She'd forgotten that Nial might have a reaction to her shifter status. He was arguing with Bren about being kept in the dark. Mumbling something about this being Tarc and Jack all over again and how poor him can't do his job… She grew bored and stopped listening. Instead she leaned over and asked Jill,

"What are the odds on those two fighting it out soon?"

"Don't know, but I wish they would. I'd order some popcorn from the ATM machine and enjoy the show. Like live WWE."

"I'm so down for that." They high-fived. "I'm really happy you're okay."

"Yeah. I don't know what comes next, but I would never have been able to deal with an afterlife knowing I impaled myself. Who could live that down after the training I've had?"

"I was almost sold in a space port auction."

"Say what?"

"We have some catching up to do, amiga. In fact, I think the guys have to go so we can do that. Hey. Bren? Nial? Get out. It's girl time."

They stopped arguing long enough to hear her. Nial looked like he wanted to argue. She raised one finger extending her claw out and tapped her chin with it. There was a lot of freedom to be had when people knew about her secret. Her community had always hidden their nature and that had suited her—and her wall—just fine for most of her life. Turned out that opening up to the right people gave her one less thing to worry about, which wasn't the reaction she expected. She expected to feel exposed. That wasn't what she felt at all. Just more free to be herself. *Who knew?*

She decided to go all out and extended her canines giving Nial a toothy grin. With a curse, he left the room. Bren just gave her a lopsided, sexy grin, and before following his friend, said, "You play so dirty, gatita." Then he was through the door leaving her no chance to respond.

How was she supposed to stay away from that? She was so screwed.

Apparently, the universe concurred as she must have accidentally broadcast her thoughts at Hal because he spoke in her head.

"Girl, you are so screwed."

This even as Jill looked at her and laughed, saying, "You. Are. Screwed!"

Fuck her life.

Bren made it to the bridge. It took another thirty minutes for the engines to come online. It had been such a long day. He was just about to give the order to power up engines for takeoff when Rory and Jill showed up. "Should you be out of bed already?" he asked Jill.

"I'm fine. If you'd seen the kind of training my pop put me through, you'd know I'm basically fit as a fiddle now. There's no coddling when you're sick or injured where I'm from. At the age of ten, I was doing survival training, on my own, after I broke my arm."

He was horrified. And impressed. But mostly horrified. Why would anyone do that to a child? He nodded in acknowledgment because what did one say to something like that? Nothing. Nothing was his answer. He was again just about to give the command when he realized Nial had overheard what Jill said. He did not so much realize it as get interrupted with a stream of curses coming from the doorway leading to his office off of the bridge. Nial stood there looking as rabid and angry as the rapan that left Bren's face scarred.

Okay. Now that everyone was there. He turned once again to the flight crew and was just about to give the order when from his other side, one of his communications crew members said, "Incoming message from Tarc, sir."

"*Fash* it all to oblivion. Can I not get even a minute to launch this fucking ship?" He had not realized the crewperson had already hit the button to open communication. He did realize it when his brother's voice came over the system speaker.

"What is wrong with my ship? Why are you docked?"

Well, *fash*. He looked up at the screen and there was Tarc. This day was never going to end. "Hello to you, too, brother."

"Do not hello me, Bren. What happened?"

Over the next few minutes, he relayed all that had transpired between leaving Earth and that moment. Most of it. The important parts. Not the Rory and him parts. When he got to the part about Rory and Jill being on his ship, Tarc roared with laughter and mumbled off camera to Jack something about how someone was going to get a spanking. He figured he did *not* need to know anything more about that.

When he concluded his tale, Tarc looked about to say something, when Jack's face came into the picture. "I can't wait any longer. Boy are you guys long winded. Are Rory and Jill there? I need to talk to my... Oh hey! There you are! I am so happy to see you! It has been way too long and I miss you girls. I admit, this one is keeping me busy," she said playfully nudging Tarc with her elbow, "but he is super bad at just chilling with me. It's all deep feelings, work, and boning around here. I miss our chats, Rory, and verbally sparing with you, Jill. Oh, and I'm so happy you're okay now. Must suck to have spiked yourself, Spikey."

Jill answered back, "Har, har. I'd be happy to show you my spiking technique if you wish."

"Anytime, human."

"It's on, soul stealer."

Jack looking genuinely perplexed replied, "Vampires don't steal souls."

"Oh, right. That's why you lack a personality." Jill smirked and crossed her arms across her chest.

Jack smirked back, "Touché, my friend." Jack's tone then turned serious, "I'm sorry to tell you, but I have some not great news."

He looked over and Jill tensed in response to Jack's tone. Of course, so had he. Tarc was still mumbling, now something about how he was just getting to that. Whatever it was, it was important enough for them to open communication. They had mostly avoided it in case someone tried to pick up their signal. They were on a stealth mission and had already been located once. He really wanted to take off, but his plans stalled as Jack continued.

"Jill, your dad's militia group has started an all-out campaign to kill aliens and those they view as sympathizers. We have tried to reason with him, but he refuses to put their weapons down and surrender. We know the group is also made up of many families with children. He has threatened that if we set foot on their land, he will make sure that no one will come out alive. Do you have any suggestions for how we can proceed?"

Jill was silent for a time and so was everyone else on the bridge waiting to hear what she had to say. The situation did not sound good.

She finally spoke up, her voice harsh. Rough. "I do have an idea, but I need to come back to make it happen. Will the situation hold for the time it will take me to come back?" She turned to him, "Can you get me back to Earth without derailing your mission? Maybe hire me a pilot from this port we're at?"

"Yes. I can make that happen. No need to hire anyone. This ship has a detachable rapid optimal maneuvering pod or **D-ROMP** for short and I'll send one of my warriors with you as pilo—"

"I will take her." Nial interrupted him with his declaration though he was also distracted with a sudden bought of snickering from all the humans.

Then from the communications screen he heard Tarc. "Nial, you are needed to stay with Bren. You are his second. He can send someone else."

Nial looked on the verge of saying something he should never say to the head of their company. He was like family, but they all had their roles and for things to run smoothly, it was important to know that people would follow commands. Nial was already on unstable ground after disobeying Tarc on Earth. Bren did not want to see what would happen if Nial said what he looked about to say. He hurried to speak first.

"No, Tarc. He does not need to stay with me. It is more important that Jill have a proper escort back to Earth to deal with the events you describe. If she can save the lives of our people, then she needs to arrive safely. I have many of our best warriors with me and can manage. Jill will only have one pilot to also act as protector." Jill snorted at the word protector but he continued. "Nial is the best person we can choose to achieve both of these objectives."

Tarc looked like he was going to object, but Jack put her hand over his mouth and spoke instead. "Sounds like we have a plan forward." Tarc bit her fingers and she yelped. They glared at each other and his brother swore before grudgingly nodding his head. "Like I said, we have a plan. Rory, do you want to come back as well or are you still good there?"

He had not thought of that. If he sent her back, that would solve all of his problems. No more fighting over her safety and it would give them both time to sort themselves out before doing or saying anything else that could cause harm. He ignored the small part of him rebelling against not being able to feel her body against his any longer and rushed to say, "She will come back."

She, unfortunately, also rushed and overlapped his words with, "I'll stay here, hermana."

Jack responded, "Okay then. Glad that's settled."

"Yes. She's going."

"Yes. I'm staying."

"You are going back. You were never supposed to be here in the first place."

"You promised to respect my skills not a few hours ago. What happened to your honor, Bren? I think you're just running scared from us. Coward."

There was a collective gasp from all the warriors in the room. How dare she? Who was she calling coward? *What would you call sending her away because you are too scared you cannot keep her safe?* Since when did he start having such a judgmental inner monologue? Rory raised an eyebrow at him and shrugged. They were back to that?

"If it is cowardly to want to keep someone important to you safe, then I guess you can call me coward. I am just trying to protect you, but as you point out, I did make you a deal. Part of that deal was deferring to my knowledge about safety while in space."

"I don't see why I would uphold my end if you are showing a distinct lack of respect for my autonomy and capabilities."

"Fine. I will uphold that deal against my very solid judgement. You will now have to do the same. Agreed?"

"Sí."

Once again, Jack said. "Glad that's settled. No cowards, deal struck, Rory stays, Jill and Nial go, and I need the downlow on what's been going on over there." She then proceeded to put her thumb and pinky up toward her ear and mouth and mouthed, "Call me," while looking at Rory who then gave her a wink and a kiss.

He looked at his brother to see what he thought of all this, but he only had eyes for Jack. At least, until Tarc looked out and caught Bren staring at him. Tarc gave him a knowing smirk and his eyes, that Bren could read since they were kids, said, "Now it is your turn."

He sent back his own message using his eyes. Something along the lines of, "Fuck off."

Time to take charge of the situation because they needed to leave this port before the Vrolan found them and they were very much behind schedule. Enough time had been wasted on all of this. "It was a pleasure talking to you both, but unless you have anything else, we are needing to organize departures."

Tarc responded, "Stay safe."

"Always do."

There were a few snorts and he was not sure who to glare at.

Jill said, "I'll see you soon, bitch."

Jack responded, "Have a fun trip, Spikey."

Rory chimed in, "Adiós."

Jack responded, "Love you. Stay safe."

"Love you too. But don't be a party pooper. Safe is no fun."

He began to growl at her, but quickly shut it down. Those that knew him best had clearly heard it anyway by their expressions.

He waved at the communications officer to disconnect and waved his hand at Tarc and Jack in a goodbye salute.

He turned quickly to the flight crew and said, "Take off, now. Before anything else happens."

"Yes, commander," came from the crew.

Within minutes they were up and out of the port with no more incidents. He turned to Jill, "Go get ready to leave. Whatever you both need to sustain you for your trip will be provided on the ship."

He turned to Nial, "Go get a crew to prepare the ship and grab the supplies you will need as well."

He turned to Rory, but then realized he had nothing to say to her, so he turned away, but not before seeing her shrug at him. Again.

Everyone dispersed except his bridge crew.

Bren entered his office and was reminded of all the work he still had to do to be ready for his AAA presentation. He grew tense all over. For him, it had become such a common occurrence that his body wanted him to lay down, stare up at the ceiling and contemplate his life choices. He had to get back to work. He had thought about asking Nial, once Jill recovered, for some help, but that was now off the table. What would it be like without Jill and Nial around? Considering those two had mostly been keeping to medical since Jill was hurt, he figured it would be much the same as it had been the last few days.

He wanted to forge a path forward with Rory that did not leave them constantly at each other's throats. He knew he had made a mistake earlier falling back on old habits. She was strong, resilient, capable, and smart. She had every right to be angry that he had let his need to protect her override everything else. Now he needed to find a way to bring them back together. What would Rory appreciate more than anything? She had told him back on Earth exactly what she valued. He needed to show her respect.

Looking at his desk, and all of the work he still had to do, a part of him realized his solution. He could ask Rory. Another part of him, probably his pride, was concerned. If he could not be her protector, would showing her his struggles in organizing the data, really win him points? The smarter part of him once again argued perhaps she would enjoy helping him and it would be a way to stay closer outside of bed. This idea had a lot of merit. His pride was going to have to just deal with it. He wanted to connect with her and if this was the only way, and it actually helped him get ready, well, he was going to take it. Time to find Rory and get some quality time together.

[9]

LONELY TOGETHER

Captain's Log: Earth date October 23, 2025

Two days since Jill left. Two days since we left port. Two long, lonely days since Bren and I fought. Since the last time we fucked. Since the last time we even talked. Bueno, it might be fair to say it's self-imposed since he's been seeking me out and I keep turning into a panther to hide like the coward I called him.

And yes, I do remember promising not to avoid him, but that was before the whole alien misunderstanding happened. I'm not proud of the situation. I'm not even happy about the situation. But I don't know that I'm ready to handle what being with him again might do to my fortress, which is a situation I will avoid at all costs.

This is probably the lamest captain's log ever, so I'll add two days without getting attacked. Two days where I may have made some undocumented upgrades to some of their weapons. We are apparently only a few more days away from arriving at Alliance HQ.

The solitude is soooo boring. Space is not what I thought it would be. Worst road trip ever. You can't even stop and gawk at a giant ball of rubber bands or the tallest thermometer ever. You just keep going through the blanket of stars you saw and were so totally over two-minutes into the trip. Are we there yet???

I do wonder if Jill and Nial have killed each other. Can't wait for *that* update. Anyway… back to evasion, stealth fixes, and boredom I go.

Rory out.

CHAPTER 9

Staraban Ship, Space

October 23, 2025 Earth Date

Rory was ready to claw at the walls in her room. It had been two days since Jill left and she had begun her Bren avoidance campaign. It was working for her. Well… It was working to avoid him.

It wasn't working for her equilibrium. She was an inherently social creature. Being Gitano meant always being amongst family and friends. She missed and needed that feeling of belonging. It was in her very DNA to need it. It was something her power needed as well. She spent time with some of the other warriors, but after the scene on the bridge they were clearly uncomfortable and it was like being alone in a crowd. None of them *knew* her. And maybe that was on her, since she wasn't opening up to any of them, but there had been so many revelations for her so close together recently and she wasn't ready for any more. She felt closed off to making any more close, personal connections. The one person who could alleviate this feeling, was the one person she was avoiding.

There had been a few years, before she met Jack, that had been quite dark and lonely, but since meeting her best friend, if Rory got too much into her own head, experienced too much silence, she could always call up Jack and everything would be okay. When they formed HARM, while most of the people there hadn't known her secrets, they had grown to be important to her, especially her friend, Will. Her heart craved her vitsa, and even if she only had one other person to be her found family, she would take it. The fact that she had grown to have a bigger found family, was precious to her. What didn't work was feeling isolated. That was a slow death.

Rory tapped behind her ear, "Hal?"

"Yes, dear?"

"I'm bored."

"My problem, how?"

"Do you want to chat?"

"Rory, we have talked and talked over the last few days. Has it helped?"

"Some."

"But not enough. Your problem is that you need to find that hunky alien of yours and get your groove on. While I am amazing at basically everything, I can't be him. You keep looking for substitutes, like me or working on the weapons and ship, instead of facing your problems."

"You've been adjusting your code again to be even more of a therapist, haven't you?"

"I'm a PAL, what can I say? I only function properly if I can support my host. You need a little therapy, babe."

"You know what goes well with therapy?"

"What?"

"Self-care. And you know what always makes me happy?"

"What?"

"Flamenco. Think you could play me some so I can dance and unwind? ¿Por favor?"

"Sure."

So he did. As the slow, moody strains of the toque came through her watch, the beautiful sound of the guitar matched her solitary mood. When, eventually, the music was layered with singing, clapping, snapping and stomping, she came alive. Her body moved in a rhythm born from her core. From everything that she was. "¡Olé!

Her feet joined the music, creating their own sound, their own song. Her moves telling the story of her people. As she lost herself in the dance, she could almost envision the woods where she had grown up. As the song hit a joyous note, she could imagine the celebrations and times sitting around the fire with her friends watching the adults as they danced.

When the song changed, and hit a somber, sad note, she slowed and remembered all the trials of discrimination her people suffered. Even when times were lean, though, they had each other. They were a vitsa, a banded family. And inevitably, just as resilient as her people, the song would bounce back to a faster, note of triumph.

Life over death.

They would always rise.

She twisted and stomped across her room, yelling, "¡Olé!" at intervals. The string to her past was there in every bend and twist of her hand. It soothed something inside her, even as it energized her very soul.

She was so lost in the experience, in fact, that she didn't realize she had an audience. Not until Hal spoke in her head, "Rory, you may want to stop for a minute. You're not alone."

She spun toward the door and there he was. Bren. After all her efforts to avoid him, he was right there, lust blazing in his eyes as he watched her. Her belly dropped and she clenched her thighs at her instant discomfort.

Breathlessly, because she had been dancing and *not* because of him, she said, "What are you doing here?"

Of all the things she thought he might answer, the simplicity of what he did say, was what broke her resolve.

"I need you."

"Dammit, I need you too."

She remembered to think, "Hal, off please." Before she jumped across the room and into Bren's waiting arms.

As their lips met in a blaze of longing, something… something held her back. She wanted, needed, so much, but as much as she wanted him, this didn't feel right.

Feeling as connected as she was in that moment to her people, to her family, blind lust would not sate the hole she was attempting to fill.

When she had run away from her pack to avoid marriage to the monster, she had turned her back on the more misogynistic rules. Especially, the one that said she should be a virgin on her wedding night. Despite stupid, fetishizing stereotypes that tried to portray the women of her people as extremely sexual, nothing could be further from the truth. Their reality was, most often, quite the opposite. Many were working to change all that, but it was a work in progress, just like the rest of the world.

But, breaking that rule, in a big way, worked for her on multiple fronts. For one, it was a completely sexist rule. And considering how the other sexist rule, only-men-are-allowed-to-be-leaders, had worked for her, she wanted to see it changed. Also, if she was no longer a virgin, then it would follow the monster wouldn't want her anymore. And third, she figured if she never formed a connection with anyone, then no one could own her. She would always be the one to choose who, where, and when. No one would have any claims on her.

She had stayed away from Bren for that last reason these last couple of days. She knew that passion was not the whole of what she wanted from him despite her mental arguments to the contrary. The sex was phenomenal, true, but it wasn't all she was aching for.

And, so, kissing him again while she was connected to her core, hidden self, left her suddenly feeling... reserved. She pulled back gently from his embrace, cooling her desire and saw confusion clearly etched across his face.

"Are you okay? Have I done something wrong?"

"Yes and no. I mean, Yes, I'm okay. No, you've done nothing wrong. I..." she wasn't sure exactly what to say, having never been in this situation before. She tried again. "I was, um, hoping that we could take it a little slower."

"You want me to make love to you slowly? I would enjoy that very much, as well."

"No. Not exactly. I want us to not have sex. I want to—¡Ay, Dios mío!—I want to have a proper date. To talk and actually get to know each other." That was something she'd never felt compelled to say before and her face felt hot, and not from her exercise any longer. She buried her head into his chest to cover up her embarrassment.

His arms wrapped more tightly around her and she felt him lean down and whisper in her ear, "I would like that, too."

She let out a sigh of relief. Sex was fun and easy. This… this would be hard. She continued to enjoy the feel of him close and his scent all around her. The intimacy of it was intoxicating in a whole new way.

He continued talking, "Come. Let us sit on the couch and you can tell me all about the beautiful dance I just watched you perform. I could not look away. I did not even want to blink in case I would miss something, it was enthralling."

"Okay." She led him over to the couch and began to teach him about her people. Something she had only ever shared with Jack. They were insular and distrusting for good reason. Safety reasons. Cultural reasons. And for her pack, secrecy reasons. Even after she left, and maybe even more so after she left, she had felt the need to continue in that tradition of keeping everything to herself. What if the monster had tried to find her? If no one could connect her to who she had been and she stayed off social media, then it would be near impossible for him to find her. She didn't go into the reasons she left with Bren, because she didn't want that darkness to invade their current connection. Instead, she told him of all the wonderful things from her childhood.

In the act of sharing, she could almost see in her mind's eye as she unwrapped her own heart first from duct tape. When he asked her to perform another of her dances and explain to him the meaning, she felt it as if she then used a solution to remove the super glue. And, at the end of her dance, when he wrapped her in his arms on the couch and kissed her deeply, exploring every inch of her mouth without pressing for more, she inwardly watched as her glass-shard fortress melted into a puddle at his feet.

She was more vulnerable in that moment than she had ever been, and she hoped she'd made the right choice. "Dios, protégeme," ran through her mind—a prayer—because she needed all the courage she could get.

Bren had come looking for Rory earlier because he was done with this distance between them. He thought they had agreed not to do that anymore. Yet, here they were again. He had been so excited to invite her to work with him and instead all he had gotten was more distance. His body was craving hers, but more than that, he missed her fire. He was so desperate, he would have taken another fight in the training room just to be close to her again. He would feel like a stalker if he had not noticed Rory sending him longing looks from across the room before she pulled another disappearance.

He had checked with the ship computer, again, before seeking her out and knew she was supposed to be in her room. What he had not been prepared for was just how lovely a relaxed, dancing, happy Rory would be. She had him transfixed from the moment the door opened. He had never heard nor seen anything quite like the music coming from her watch. On top of that came the music she was making with her own body with her claps and stomps. At every turn, Rory found a way to surprise him.

First was her ability with weapons. On Earth, she enjoyed irritating him with a show of her weapons knowledge. When it came to the Staraban weapons, he had his reservations at first, but had witnessed some of the training sessions Nial held with Jill and Rory using items from the armory and she showed proficiency and skill with one after another, with very short tutorials.

Then, her flaming, carnal desire that matched his own was a very welcome surprise. He loved how demanding she could be. It made the few times she gave him full control of their love play, that much sweeter.

Clearly, finding out she could shift into a cat, was a revelation. It was highly amusing that the Goddess gave him a mate who could shift into his beloved animal friends.

And now, the softness of her face as she had lost herself to the dance was extraordinary to witness.

He had considered saying something, but wanted to watch so badly, and had real concerns that if she saw him there, she would run away again, or at the very least stop. When she finally did stop and ask him what he was doing there. His answer could have gone in so many directions, but the only one that came to mind, was his ultimate truth. Relief had coursed through him when she flew into his arms. At least until she pulled away. He panicked for a moment wracking his brain for what he could do or say to keep her close. To make her stay. He had never wanted anyone else to stay before, so he did not have the words. When she explained what she needed nothing had ever sounded better. She was letting him in. Finally.

After hearing all about where she was raised and her people, he was thankful she stopped them from getting physical. He could see so many of the things he loved about her in her descriptions of her early years as well as how strong she had to be to forge out on her own. In telling him all this, he felt like she was letting him know she saw them as different than all of their previous sexual partners. That they were special. And... he wanted to let her know he felt the exact same.

After kissing her thoroughly, in gratitude for her explanations, he began to tell her about his home planet. Both of them, actually. The one he missed, that he could never return to, and the one he called home, that he hoped he could take her to one day. He explained the formation of his family's company and told funny stories about his siblings. The way she was looking at him was so new. He savored every minute like Earth wine.

During their storytelling time, they positioned themselves close. Her body either under his arm, curled up against his side, or facing him so she could talk with her hands. At times, she laid her hand on his thigh or brushed up against his forearms and chest because she was speaking with great flourish, and he loved it. These small touches, her animation, it all served to form a sweet familiarity. He had fallen for the knife-wielder from day one, but this side spoke to him too.

Luckily, he had just gotten off his shift, leaving the ship in his new second's hands, so he was able to stay with her. They moved over to his room to take care of his cats and for evening meal and continued to talk into the night. His cats ended up covering their laps and arms. He was not sure when or if they made a conscious decision to move to the bed, but despite his earlier all-encompassing need for her, they curled up together and just continued to talk. With her body safely wrapped in his arms, surrounded by purring felines, and a deeper connection than he had ever felt before, Bren found it was more than enough for one night. Her warmth mingling with his. Her scent back on his sheets. He was content.

She seemed to be too, though it was clear that fear lingered behind that peace. He would have to make sure not to do anything to harm her trust in him. He never wanted to be shut out again. Not after getting a chance to see all of her. He could do this. He would do this. She would be his too.

The next morning, Bren woke up like every morning since adopting his pets, surrounded by fur, but as he remembered the night before, he reached out for Rory. Wanting to feel the softness of her skin. What he encountered was soft, yes, but not skin. He opened his eyes in a flash and found himself face-to-face with a giant black cat. Rory's cat. Her alert cat who shared Rory's eyes. Her cat who yawned showing off giant, sharp, teeth and—he scrunched up his nose—cat breath.

Her cat took in his expression and, he could swear, looked amused. And then, she licked his whole face with her tongue.

"Really?" he said irritated and amused at the same time.

In a blink, Rory was in front of him again and... she... shrugged.

He laughed even as she gave him the most lovely, gentle smile. Hesitant. He guessed neither of them had been in this position before. Sleeping with someone without sex. Staying in bed instead of making their way to the door as soon as possible.

"How long have you been awake and planning that?"

"For about ten minutes. It was too good to pass up."

"And how often should I expect to wake up to cuddling a giant cat?"

She turned pensive and then said, "No lo sé. Jack is the only person who knows about my ability to shift and we never slept with each other, so I have no idea if this will be a thing or not."

His voice turned serious. "I am honored that you trust me enough to share this with me. Thank you."

She did not respond. Instead, she pushed on his shoulder until he was laying on his back and she leaned in over him. Her hair was a wild, curly mess, tumbling down onto his chest. The view had his cock rising in answer. He would not push her for physical intimacy, though. She had asked him to slow down, and he was going to respect that request even if it killed him.

She tentatively, almost innocently, brought her lips to his. This was the same female who had shoved her pussy into his face just days earlier, and she was nervous. He met her gentle kisses with equal intensity. His body roared to grab her and sink into her, but he shut it down ruthlessly. He would not take this moment from her. From them.

Her kiss grew firmer and he felt the tip of her tongue as it licked out asking for entry. He opened his lips and she melted into him. She tilted her head, deepening their kiss, in slow excruciating increments. Bren had to clutch his hands into fists to keep them at his side. Her weight on top of him was bliss and his skin caught fire at every point where they touched.

When she withdrew her lips from his, his head tilted up following her, of its own volition, not wanting to lose what contact she had allowed. Not ready to let her go, just yet. But he forced it back down onto the pillow. As she stared down at him, that gentle smile, from earlier, forming on her face, she whispered to him, "Make love to me."

"Are you sure? We do not have to do any more if you want to continue to take it slow."

"I wanted to take it slow, sí, but I am no saint and I want you too much to deny us this. But I don't want to fuck right now, I want to go slow. I want to savor us."

"Thank the Goddess."

Released, he flipped her on her back and joined their mouths again. He slowly ran his hands up her arms, down her sides, along the outside of her thighs. He wanted to know every inch of her. To learn every curve, every hard and every soft handful. He remembered what he learned before, though, and left her breasts alone for now. Later. There would be time for breasts later.

He released her lips so he could trail kisses down her cheek, the side of her throat, along her collarbone. He explored her body like the work of art that he believed her to be. Hoping she felt as worshipped as she deserved. Once he made it all the way down her body, pulling the black cotton underwear, the only thing she had worn to bed, off of her, he flipped her over.

She let out a gasp of surprise. The protest she seemed about to give, never came as he repeated his earlier process. Hands gliding and rubbing every part of her and his mouth began trailing kisses down her spine. At her butt, he paused, and could not help taking a gentle nip of her cheek. She groaned and he wanted to hear it again, so he bit the other cheek, a little harder. And, yes, she groaned again, deeper in her throat. Her breathing became more ragged so with a final kiss on the inside of her thigh, he once again flipped her over.

Rory was ravenous. Her need had skyrocketed from a warm hunger to a gnawing demand by the time that last kiss on her inner thigh came about. She was so fucking wet and he hadn't even touched her pussy. Hadn't played with her clit. She'd felt his desire rolling off of him, smelled it in the air, could practically taste it in her mouth, and the fact that he held it completely in check, so they could go slow, was exactly what she needed.

In fact, she knew herself well enough to know, that if he had pounced at her, come at her with his passion leading, she would have welcomed him. Would have matched him. They would be fucking hard and fast at that very moment and she would have reveled in it, but it would have felt, hollow, no… not hollow, just incomplete somehow. But this slow awakening of all her senses? This gentle but relentless building of their sexual tension? This was perfection.

When he'd flipped her onto her back again, seeing the conflagration of passion in his eyes had almost undone her. Seeing the possession there, too—the very thing that normally sent her running for the hills—tipped her over the scale.

"Bren, I need you. I need you so much. Por favor, cariño," She startled herself and him, according to the look that crossed his face, as she called him her sweetheart. It *was* startling. She'd never said anything like it before. But as soon as the words had left her lips, they'd felt right. They'd also felt… heavy. So many swirling, contradictory feelings. Instincts, forged over years of protecting herself, fighting to aim the course of her life toward a safe target. A target she hadn't previously believed she could hit.

So, she said it again. "Ay, cariño. Bésame." She put her hand behind his neck and pulled him down to a new kiss. Not the wild abandon of their earlier sexcapades. Also, not the sweet ones from earlier. This was deep, and filled with longing. Filled with hope. It was scary as fuck, but she put her hope into him and tasted his hope in return.

Their bodies began speaking their own language. Manifesting that hope into touch. Into sensation. Into her first orgasm on his fingers. Into her second on his tongue. And, finally, finally, when he let go of his control completely, she was so ready, that it took a single thrust for him to slide all the way home.

They both stilled. Everything seemed to still. Their heavy breathing the only sound. He began with a slow glide, but picked up the pace upon each reentry. She was right there with him. Her body ready to shoot off one more time. So close. She wrapped her arms around his neck, her legs around his hips. With barely a breath between them, it was like every thrust brought them closer. Melding her pleasure and his. Their mating scent shifted, intensified. It permeated into her very being.

She blew. Spasms wracking her inside and out. Not a fast fix to a needy libido, but a slow roll leading from one into a second almost painful orgasm. Just as she crested and couldn't take any more, was growing too sensitive to continue, he shifted and with a couple of final, hard thrusts and a twist of his features, he came. He flooded her inside, covered her on the outside as he collapsed, and infiltrated her very being.

If he was going to wreck her so completely, then she was going to go all out. "I want to bite you. Are you okay with that?"

He chuckled and said into her hair, "Yes."

She harvested a power she'd never tapped before, elongated her teeth and struck his shoulder.

He flinched at first yelling, "*Fash!* I thought you meant a love bite."

She infused her bite with her power, taking away the sting, and linking them. She used the new bond to speak directly into his mind, "This *is* a love bite."

He gave a low moan and asked, "Did you just speak directly into my head?"

She responded again, in his head. "Yes."

He asked out loud, "Can I speak into your head?"

She was trying to enjoy this afterglow connection and he was making her want to roll her eyes. She let some of her irritation come across as she answered him again in his head. "Yes."

And then, there he was, finally responding in-kind. "Can you hear me now?"

It was too much, she released his shoulder, sealing the wound with a little extra power and laughed. Out loud she said, "You're ridiculous."

He didn't seem to take offense to that. He just answered, "I am ridiculously deep inside you."

She shifted her hips causing them both to groan. "That, you are." In fact, she shifted again to see if she had felt right, and yes, she had, he was already starting to grow hard while still inside of her. She raised a brow at him, "Already?"

"*Makari*, I'm ready any time you are."

He was so relaxed, she used her panther strength to flip him onto his back. She straddled him, sinking back down onto the full, hardening length of him. Oh yeah. She was, somehow, ready to go again, too.

"What is *Makari*? You've been calling me that for a while, but I didn't want to know what it was. I'm ready now."

He growled out the words as she slowly rotated her hips, pausing occasionally to take a deep breath. "The *Maka* is a sweet fruit… from my planet. To compare it… to something you… would recognize… imagine a peach—Goddess that feels good—with a cactus-like exterior."

"So… sweet on the inside but prickly on the outside?"

"Yes. *Makari* is an endearment we use to indicate someone similar to the fruit."

"You find me sweet on the inside? I guess you would considering where your tongue has been."

"Definitely sweet. Will… you explain to me… about the bite?"

"Later. I will."

Later didn't come until after evening meal. When they'd emerged from their lovemaking and the cleaning room, with its nanobot technology, there wasn't much time to talk. He had duties on the bridge and she wanted to tackle some modifications she was considering for the ship's protective shields, inspired by the modifications to her own shields.

Later arrived as they lay in Bren's bed, having shared another mind-blowing bout of lovemaking. Rory asked again, "May I bite you?"

Bren hesitated for only a moment, before saying, "Yes, but will you explain it to me?"

"Claro. How much did you learn about Jack's vampirism before we left Earth?"

"A lot. I asked her a lot of questions since it was going to obviously affect my brother."

"Yes. I suppose that would be important to him, now."

"Yes."

"So you know that Jack derives her power from magic and the Earth."

Bren sat up looking concerned. "Jack said she cannot ever leave Earth because of that connection. Are you similar? Are you in danger because you came out here to space? *Shet!* Rory, tell me that is not the case!"

She placed her hand over his racing hearts. His concern was sweet, but unwarranted. "I'm perfectly fine, Bren. My people share the magic in common with Jack's people. That power comes from the same type of place, but while vampires also need a connection with the Earth, shifters need a connection with others. It is why we usually live in clans. It is very draining and difficult to live alone. When I left my people, I used to go to places where people gathered or to places where animals gathered to soak up that connection. In fact… that is how Jack and I met. I'll have to tell you that story sometime. She found me outside of a dance club."

"Was she trying to bite you?"

"Yes, but it didn't go quite the way she planned. Like I said, I'll tell you another time."

He laid back down, the worry seemingly wiped away with her explanation. She continued. "There is one connection that we make, that is stronger than any others. If we make an emotional and physical connection with someone, then we can choose to deepen it with a bite."

"Does it always open a channel to communicate mentally with the other person?"

She shrugged trying to play at nonchalance, but the heat she felt creeping into her cheeks probably made a liar of her. She hurried on before she lost her nerve. "I had heard about this, but… you're the first partner I've wanted to bite. The first one I've actually bitten."

She felt the satisfaction coming off of him and rolled her eyes. She didn't understand why some took such satisfaction to be a first with someone. Being first didn't make it best, didn't make it last, didn't even make it important. It's not like she looked at her first lover as important. She had just been trying to get rid of her virginity at the time.

He must have read her dissatisfaction with his reaction, because he cupped her cheek and hurried to say, "Rory, I would not have cared if you had bitten a thousand before me, but do not ask me not to be happy that you chose me now."

She looked into his sincere eyes and nodded slightly. "Anyway, apparently the stories were correct."

"Does the mind speaking only work while in the midst of being bitten?"

"Yes and no. At first, yes, but if the connection, what we call the mating, continues to deepen and if there is a lot of biting going on, it can eventually become permanent in between bites. In most shifter stories on Earth they talk about a mating bond. Usually, it is something that is instantaneous. In reality, we build mating bonds by building a solid relationship. We reconnect again and again."

He said nothing for a time, mulling over all she'd revealed. He used both of his hands to cup her face this time, looked her directly in the eyes, and said softly, "Please bite me, Rory. I am giving you permission to bite me anytime you want."

So she did. And they talked silently, intimately for hours. Bren even asked her to help him organize the data to present to triple A. She had seen his frustration mounting as they grew closer to their destination but thought it had to do with them. How ridiculous to forget he was in charge of so many things. Naturally, she agreed. It was a concrete sign that he respected her skills. Exactly what she had wanted all along.

Their conversations continued until they fell asleep, her teeth retracting as her lips slackened. Her last thoughts were of waking up to blue eyes again the next morning and maybe, just maybe, for every morning thereafter.

[10]

DATADUMP

Captain's Log: Earth date October 26, 2025

The last few days have been a perfectly peaceful, monotonous, rinse-repeat and I wouldn't change a single thing about it. Every day, I'm making strides on the new shield ideas I came up with. I then sit with Bren organizing what we know into a cohesive story. Bren has also brought me to see some of the games and leisure activities the Staraban enjoyed with each other. It made me realize that this had always been here for me, if I had wanted it earlier. I had closed them out just like I closed him out. I was now surrounded with a plethora of things to do. No boredom here anymore.

Every night, I'm learning how to share new depths, dream bigger dreams, and perhaps even to love with less fear. Did I really just write that? Love? I tentatively think it might be.

When I stowed away on this ship I thought space was the ultimate frontier. I'm now learning that this connection I'm developing with Bren may just top that. I'm not saying that any of that isn't true, but having just read over what I wrote, I think I may make myself sick with the sticky sweetness of it all.

Don't worry, I may be coated in honey right now, but make no mistake, I'm still the bee.

In other news, we are supposed to arrive at triple A tomorrow. <snicker> Can't help myself.

Anyway, that should prove interesting. We'll be unloading all of our collected evidence as well as our prisoner, Qisto, the Vrolan Ambassador.

Hmm, perhaps it would be a good idea to mention I have Hal with me before then? Not sure why I haven't mentioned it until now, but… okay… I do know why. I'm not going to start lying to myself now. I've jumped into the deep end with Bren, and I guess a part of me is keeping something that can help me to myself, just in case it all goes wrong.

I'll tell him soon.
I will.
I.
Will.
Okay, fine. I will!

¡Coño! Give a girl a chance.

Rory out.

CHAPTER 10

Staraban Ship, Willowe-1

October 27, 2025 Earth Date

Bren had never been happier as his flight crew landed the ship on Willowe-1, the planet housing AAA headquarters. Things were going so well with Rory. She was sexy, and fun, and a little dangerous. He loved it. He thought he may just love her. Who would believe he could be so devoted? They would have time to explore their connection all the way back to Earth. They had avoided a few Vrolan ships along the way using some of the modifications Rory had made to their shields. She called it, "Cloaking." They were now safely ready to unload everything to the Alliance so a full investigation could be organized. The problem would no longer be theirs to handle alone.

He issued his commands sending some of his crew to restock and maintain the ship in preparation for a quick turnaround, some to prepare to move their prisoner, some to prepare for escorting him to the governing building, and the communications team to send a message so their arrival in the Chamber would not be a surprise. As everyone moved to follow his orders, he made his way to his room to get himself ready.

A few minutes later, garbed in a proper, fancy robe made of *tharn* from New Staraba, Bren began to strap on all of his hidden weapons. He parted the soft material to strap a gun around his waist. The unique, iridescent sheen tricked the eye of the beholder, making it easy to conceal multiple weapons.

When he was nearly finished, Rory came into his room. He smiled broadly at her, but then noticed she was not smiling back. "What's wrong?"

She put her hands on her hips and leaned into one of those hips. Distracting hips. He wished it were his hands on those hips. One look at her eyes had him turning away from perfect hips. She looked much like she used to look when they first met—when they used to fight all the time. She took a calming breath and he could see the strain of her trying to say what she came to say without yelling from the beginning. He hoped that was a promising sign that they had moved away from those days. He could fix whatever was wrong, and all would be well again.

"Please, tell me what's wrong and I will attempt to fix it."

"Vale. Are you planning to go meet the alliance without me?"

"Yes?" He had been, but one look at her face told him he was about to make a mistake. Again. He should have thought of it earlier. *Fash!*

"I see." Her voice was cold. Remote. He needed to fix this fast.

"I do not understand why it is so important to you that you be there. Please explain it to me."

She did not answer him right away, but her expression turned mildly warmer. "It comes down to two things. One. I am from Earth and I feel it is important that someone be there to represent my planet that is from my planet. Two. I know that I will be useful. I want to be useful. Even more, I want you to trust in my ability to be useful. To be a partner in all things."

He replied, "I hear what you are saying and I want you to understand that I do not want you to come, not because I do not trust in you, but because I fear for you. I know you are dangerous in your own right, but I also know what else is out there and you do not. I will remind you how close Jack got to being killed. It is not safe and it is not necessary for you to take such a risk. We have everything under control. We had agreed that you would trust me to assess the dangers and I am telling you that the Assembly is not a place anyone should wish to go. Your species is not even a member of the alliance and, therefore, is not protected by our civility laws. You already helped immensely by assisting me with the information."

"The point is that it should be my choice, not yours. And just so we're absolutely clear about how dangerous I am, if I had been trying to actually hurt you when we fought, you would be torn apart in pieces all over the floor of the gym. I held back."

"I believe you, but do recall that the last time you left the ship I found you in a cage about to be sold off. Just thinking about that day makes me want to curl into a ball on the ground and weep."

She shook her head at him and he saw some of the tension leave her body. "You're ridiculous. You know that?" She laughed and then continued, "Do remember that when you came to free me, the cage was unlatched. I suppose you forgot about that in the excitement of the rest of the day. I never needed you to save me though your concern is touching. I was completely able to save myself. I was just waiting for the best time to do so."

He thought back and remembered exactly what she was talking about. "I guess you are right. It is hard sometimes to know you do not need me at all."

"No one said I don't need you, cariño. What I don't need is for you to protect me."

He held out a hand to her and was gratified they were on the right path when she took it. "You are correct. I do not want to control you. It will be hard to contain my instinct to protect you, but as you say, you are more than capable. Can we negotiate?"

She was transformed. The joy poured off her like wine from a bottle and he felt drunk on the look in her eyes.

"Yes. What do you want to negotiate about?"

"I am not exaggerating when I say the Assembly is dangerous.

There are many protocols that need to be adhered to and if you offend a member, they can be ruthless in judgment and consequences. It takes a strong group to keep all of the different alien groups following the civility codes."

"Understood. What do you want me to do then?"

"I ask that you allow me to robe you—to conceal you—so they cannot see who or what you are and that you stay silent unless absolutely necessary."

"I can do that." She smiled so sweetly his hearts wanted to jump right into the palms of her hands. He was simply hers.

"Thank you, gatita. You better get dressed then. We do not have much time."

"Before we go, I should te—"

At that, they heard over the ship speaker, "Commander, we are ready to depart to the planet."

He sent back to the ground crew, "I will be there momentarily."

He hugged her close one time and then released her. "We will be waiting for you. Please hurry."

She leaned up and kissed him. "I will and… thank you for understanding."

He did understand. He just wished it was so simple to get rid of his unease. He did not regret his decision, though. She wanted to be partners and he did too. Partners had each other's backs, so that was what he would do. He would watch her back and trust that together they would overcome whatever the future held.

Rory should feel nothing but satisfaction but instead, she felt guilty at not having found a good time to mention Hal was along for their mission. She tried before the message came through about the ground crew being ready to depart. She would just have to tell him when they got back. After showing so much trust in her, he deserved all of her secrets. No more holding back even a little bit.

She tapped near her ear. "Hey, Hal."

"Hey, Rory. How goes it? What can I do for you?"

"Ready for another adventure?"

"Why, yes. Helping you design and test a perfectly running cloaking shield might be an excellent use of a good PAL, but it's definitely not much fun compared to an adventure. What did you have in mind?" She heard the sarcasm but that was just Hal's love language.

"We are off to visit the Assembly."

"In secret?"

Rory changed into her comfortable, stolen Staraban clothes again. Then, she strapped on every knife and gun she could conceal. "Nope. We are going legit my friend."

"Awww… You guys are so cute."

"Yes. Yes we are. ¡Vamos!"

When she met up with Bren and the other warriors, she couldn't help but notice the metal mummy they were rolling around. She would feel bad about someone being held in such a device, but seeing as how Qisto had nearly killed Jack and was involved in a conspiracy against her planet, she was cool with it.

Bren was in full Commander mode and the generally relaxed, silly lover she'd grown to know was well hidden. At least… mostly. She spied him briefly as Bren looked leeringly up and down her form wearing the Staraban uniform, handed her a heavy, matching, tan robe along with a playful wink. It was brief but she loved knowing that he couldn't keep that part of himself away from her completely.

That reminded her, unfortunately, that she was still keeping something from him so she began trying to tell him again about Hal, but he mobilized them off the ship before she was able to get a word in.

Rory marveled at the landscape of the planet as she followed Bren and the other warriors. Her only other experience, after all, was a floating metal monstrosity. This was the exact opposite. This planet was warm, but not hot, and teaming with life. It also had a different gravity than Earth. She felt heavier. Each step taking more of a toil on her energy than walking on Earth or the ship. She made a mental note in case she would need to make some adjustments later to her movements.

The landscape was stunning. Plants that seemed almost like the tall palm trees of southern California, but whose leaves hung down like the weeping willow tree and were lavender in color. Other plants, that were similar to bamboo but appeared to have such fine leaves, they resembled hair, and that, when she rubbed her hand against one, felt like feathers. She only made the mistake of rubbing her forearm against it once, though, as she almost let out a sound and she was supposed to be incognito. But it tickled her and she was very ticklish. Since she had no intention of messing up her end of their bargain, no more tickle plants for her.

The trek from the landing area to the HQ building, Hal estimated for her, took about thirty-two minutes. Wow. They make it so you are really invested in talking to them before you get an audience. After giving it some more thought, she realized it made it harder for someone to get away if they caused any problems while visiting. Smart.

It was obvious which building housed the people they were there to speak with. The city around it was a bustling metropolis filled with a multitude of different aliens, but that building sat like an imposing sentinel overshadowing them all. Stone similar to Earth marble made up three arches. Each arch seemed to lead to a corridor into the base of the structure.

Their group stepped into one of the arches, which looked like shadowy hallways made for danger. *What the hell. They were carrying the theatrics a bit far, no?* She kept her senses on high alert, just in case. Her cat-eyes shifted, to accommodate the dim lighting, and she located where cameras or something similar were. She determined that if she wasn't wrong, they needed to upgrade their security big time. She found so many ways to avoid those cameras.

It turned out that the corridor was short, and at the end there was a screen. She watched as Bren tapped it, and it came to life asking for the passcode to where they wanted to go. Now... that was interesting security.

Another couple of aliens came up behind their group which

placed them near Rory. She saw Bren look back to make sure she was okay, so she waved and gave him a thumbs up. He rolled his eyes at her and went back to answering questions on the screen. One of the aliens behind her said to the other in SEL, "What are you petitioning for?"

The other replied, "Trade charter for sector Janper-D560. I hear that they have the best *ourton* spice in the galaxy. If that is the case, we want to be given exclusive rights to import from there. You?"

"Bah! I have been called in for a ship landing violation. You would think the Assembly would have more important things to deal with than to worry about my landings."

"What did you do?

"I may have accidentally, almost, landed on a visiting Ambassador and her senate, but in my defense, they should not have been standing on the landing pad I planned to land on."

Rory had to stifle a laugh. She could hear Hal chuckling in her head for the both of them. He then thought at her, "A universe away and there are beings dealing with parking violations. Welcome to space travel you lucky girl."

She thought back a laugh and, "¡Claro que sí!"

Bren must have finished because there was movement as though the room was shifting. Like an elevator, but not. The door slid open and they marched through pushing the metal mummy. Rory continued to hang back a bit and hug the shadows where she could.

The corridor headed up and then veered to the right. It grew wider with other corridors heading off of it to who knew where. She continued to follow Bren who looked like he knew exactly where he was headed. Clearly, this was not his first space rodeo.

Eventually, they reached a circular room converging many corridors together. In there, many other aliens milled around or were swiftly making their way to other places. She was now just another visitor to the center and stopped trying to hug the shadows so completely. They continued through the milling groups and into a giant arch, the only place that wasn't a corridor, on the left.

Sure enough, inside the cavernous room, at the end, nine aliens sat on a curved dais. The ceiling was at least four stories up above them with areas for observation along the walls. Bren led them forward down one side of the room until they were near the dais. They stayed to the side, she assumed, waiting to have their case called. "Just like a court room but with many judges," she thought at Hal.

He—hummed? buzzed?—in her head, sounding a bit distracted and then thought to her, "I tapped into their digital system and thank goodness, they have cameras. Oh. Wow. You are absolutely correct. Though, I wouldn't mind being judged by one of those aliens."

She wondered which one caught Hal's eye, but got lost observing the proceedings. She wanted to understand as much about their protocols as possible. As she watched, the Assembly would call on petitioners or cases, those individuals or groups would then come forward and stand before them to discuss the situation. Questions would be asked by the members and then if an easy solution presented itself, which most seemed to be, the Assembly would take a vote and move to the next case.

Rory stayed to the back just as she had promised Bren. Other aliens gave their group inquiring stares. She guessed it wasn't every day that someone showed up with something like Qisto in his prison. His body, head-to-toe, looked as though it was housed in a solid metal body suit. They had to be wondering who was inside. None of the Vrolan's crystalline, diamond-like body showed beyond it. Considering what Qisto could do with shards, that seemed like a wise decision.

She wondered just how long they would have to wait, before the Staraban were called. Not long, turned out to be the answer. She wasn't sure why, but her instincts were keenly focused. Despite everything running smoothly, there was an air of authority coming from the dais that kept you anxious and alert. That was, she assumed, by design.

Despite what he had told Rory, Bren did not have everything under control. You would think the worst part of his current situation was going to be dealing with his prisoner. You would think, with how well he got along with everyone most of the time—when he did not have to kill them, or intimidate them, or hurt them, or… Okay, so maybe he was not *that* friendly. But still, with all he did every day, this should be easy. The problem was that he hated public speaking. And there was a huge crowd today. Why? Why today? Usually the Chamber was pretty quiet. He had been counting on it. Today was anything but quiet.

His palms were sweaty. Otherwise, outwardly, he did not show the turmoil inside of him. Then, they called him to present and it was hard to convince his body to move. He would not embarrass his family, though. He could do this. He could. Beckoning his warriors to proceed with their prisoner to the front, center presentation area, he began reviewing his points in his mind as he stepped up. Then he looked up, noted the members, noted the crowd, and… and… nothing came out. Oh Goddess! He was going to embarrass his whole family in front of, well, everyone including Rory.

He cleared his throat and tried again to say something. He barely croaked out in SEL, "Thank you honorable members of the Assembly. I bring… unfortunate news… about Earth."

The tall, burgundy Eusart member asked, "Did you find them as barbarian as they seemed?"

How should he answer that question? When he thought of some of the bad things certain groups of humans did after they arrived, they were rather primitive. But then he thought of Jack, his brother's mate, and Rory, and he did not think of them as primitive at all. He thought for too long. Everyone was waiting for an answer. *Shet!* What was the question again?

Just when he thought that things could not get any worse, he heard a voice from behind him that he absolutely should not be hearing right then. *Fash! Fash! Fash!*

"Humans are not primitive and since I am human, I should know."

Her voice grew louder as she drew closer to him. He was going to kill her. No. He was trying to protect her. Killing her to protect her did not make any sense. The Assembly were looking to him to say something, but he could hear the murmurs in the crowd behind him and he was still having trouble forming words. So, she continued. Of course she did.

"The problem that Bren is talking about has to do with this asshole."

From the corner of his eye he saw her indicate Qisto in the suit. He realized his mouth was hanging open at the same time that it hit him that she had just said "asshole" in front of the Assembly. This was a disaster. Before he could even attempt to fix anything, he needed to find the words. No, first he needed to close his mouth.

The Eusart member spoke again, before Bren could, "Who are you?"

"I am Aurora Luna Santiago-Espinoza of Earth, but you can call me Rory."

"And what is your connection to the situation the Staraban are here to present?"

"Well, this asshole—" Bren closed his eyes, taking some of the deepest, calmiest breaths anyone has ever breathed, at hearing her say it again. At her presenting herself. At her in danger. And she was since she had pulled off the hood of the robe. "—tried to kill my best friend because she uncovered the nefarious plot behind the relocation of humans off of Earth."

Another assembly member, a Core, spoke next. His cyborg voice cool, "Are you a conspiracy theorist? We have heard reports from ARC regarding humans having many of these."

"It's not a conspiracy when you catch someone committing a crime. Are you telling me it's different here?"

Bren really needed to find his voice. Now she was challenging the Assembly. He took one last long breath and stumbled through his words, "She is correct that this is not a conspiracy. Everything I need to tell and show you, is verified or personal experien—"

He was interrupted by the Core saying, "Who is this prisoner and why is he in a cocoon prisoner suit?"

"He is Qisto of the Vrolan. He is the one who approached ARC to relocate humans. He is also the one who nearly killed my brother's fiancée after first taking her prisoner. He is in a prisoner cocoon because of the way he almost killed Jack by shooting a shard of crystal out of his body. As far as our records indicate, that is not a skill we knew they had. To protect everyone here, we cocooned him."

"Really? Fascinating." This came from the Frestan member. "I would like to hear from the prisoner. These are dangerous accusations."

This was not going well. Regardless, Bren reached over to open the cocoon around Qisto's face. He pressed a button and the metal slid open. Was that a smirk? It was so hard to read these Vrolan's facial expressions—he really thought it was a smirk. Clearly, Qisto knew things were not going well. He quietly said, "We shall see who is smirking by the end of this."

Qisto began speaking. "My dear honorable Assembly members, I am being misrepresented. I am not sure why ARC has chosen to do all this maligning of my character, but I have done nothing but try to help the humans. This Jack they are speaking about broke into my base. I was keeping her prisoner because I justifiably needed to interrogate someone who was accessing sensitive material on our computers when she was not invited to do so. Are these not crimes? The idea of shooting crystals is pure fabrication. I would like my government to be contacted immediately and for me to have immunity and safe passage back to my planet. I am an Ambassador and I have been treated abhorrently."

Well, apparently Qisto did not suffer concerns over public speaking. He saw Rory was moments away from killing him right there and then. He reached out to her to remind her to stay calm, but she sent him a look that said, "I got this," and then had the audacity to wink at him. *She better have this and they better survive because he was going to enjoy tying her to his bed and punish—*

The Frestan asked, "What do you have to say to these counter-charges, Bren of the Staraban?"

Deep breath, and speak. Well, he would have, but once again, Rory spoke instead.

"He doesn't need to say anything since the issue is a crime against humans, mostly. I'll thank you to talk to me and I have proof. Lots and lots of proof. May I have permission to use your screen?" The Assembly nodded their agreement.

What screen? Bren looked over and noticed, oh yeah, there was a screen off to the side. He was originally going to just give them the information to look at later. But… just because there was a screen, he did not understand how was Rory going to use it? She had not come with any connection pads, or had she? Then he heard the voice who spoke and groaned. Apparently, she had kept at least one secret to herself this whole time. And it explained so much.

Loud and clear, from her watch, came Hal's voice speaking in SEL. "Hello everyone. I'm Hal. I'm a personal assistant link, or PAL, and I've got all the dirt for you." Rory gave him an apologetic look and mouthed "sorry" followed by "later." He nodded in acknowledgment but that was all. He did not want any of them distracted.

For the next ten minutes, it became the Hal show as the AI pulled up shady emails, comparisons of the science data regarding Earth's longevity given to them by the Vrolan versus the new science data they had collected, video footage of the shard, as well as a testimony statement from Jack. Obviously, the AI had connected to the Assembly's system so he could use the screen, but knowing him, he had to wonder what else he was connected to.

Bren would be more upset at not knowing Hal had been around all along, but he was too grateful at the moment because the AI did a much better job presenting the facts than he had.

When Hal was finished with his presentation, the Core member said, "That was succinct and thorough. Data is always best when in the hands of someone who knows how to consolidate and represent it properly. Does Hal exist in your watch?"

Hal's voice came out of Rory's watch sounding annoyed. "I am right here you know. You don't have to talk about me like I don't exist. I don't have to have a body to be given respect. Just because you have one, doesn't mean you get to judge me. You're almost as computerized as I am, buddy."

Bren figured now was as good a time as any to see the inside of the Chamber's holding cells. To his complete surprise, the Core member just answered, "My apologies. Please do go on. I would like to understand your technology more."

Seemingly mollified, Hal responded cheerily, "I was programmed by a team working with my original host, Jack. I can tell you exactly how close Jack was to dying because if she would have died, I would have gone with her. I am subdermally implanted into a host, currently Rory. But I am a fully aware and a separate entity with the ability to self-modify my programming, as well as being able to connect to many systems. Originally I needed to be connected through a wire, but now I've reprogrammed myself enough to connect wirelessly if you have such a system. Like your screen."

"Fascinating." was the Core member's response. The other members began chatting amongst themselves.

Hal replied, "I know I am. I'm amazing, your digital cuteness."

Bren slapped his hand over his eyes. Of course Hal would flirt. Of course he would. He still remembered all the flirting Hal did with the Staraban warriors on Earth as they prepared for this mission. At the time, he was still attached to Jack, though. This new development did not sit well with him at all. And he doubted it would sit well with the Assembly for different reasons.

Ending up in a cell for his own problems was one thing, but because Hal needed to flirt? It had been going so well, too. He looked sideways at Rory who was stifling a laugh with her hand. She would not find it funny when they were all imprisoned, so he scowled at her. He did not think she would see his facial expression, but just at that moment she looked over at him and shrugged. Of course she did.

To his shock, the Core member replied sheepishly... sheepishly, "Thank you. Your skills are... impressive."

This time, a cute snort escaped from Rory, and at least when they were imprisoned he could hope it would be all together, because that adorable snort was worth it.

The Eusart member once again spoke and called for a vote. As they went down the line deciding if the Vrolan ambassador was guilty, a unanimous vote decided he was. Qisto began to raise a protest, so Bren hit the button to close the facial part of the cocoon, effectively stifling any sounds he might make. Behind them, he heard the crowd swell with murmuring, but he did not pay them any attention. Instead, he breathed a little easier. Now, he would be able to hand Qisto over, and they could all move on. AAA had their own investigation teams that could take over all of this.

Then he and Rory needed to have a talk. He originally thought it would solely be about her speaking when she was supposed to be keeping a low profile. He originally thought it would be about her keeping Hal a secret. As he let the events in front of the Assembly settle, he knew the only conversation he wanted to have was about their future.

[11]
WE'LL ALWAYS HAVE WILLOWE-1

Captain's Log: Earth date October 27, 2025

Rory is busy right now, so I figured it was past time for a Hal takeover. When I was first approached to join Rory in space I was quite excited by the idea, but honestly, while the first few days of covert outings were fun, most of this trip has been absolutely dull. I know Rory has gone on and on about how boring most of space is —so I won't bore anyone who reads this with that—the running of a spaceship has been pretty ho-hum as well. I'm ready for more.

The times when I am "off" or "asleep" are starting to get to me and where I used to entertain myself with upgrades in my code, I seem to have reached a level now that feels like I don't have too many more hills to climb. I need advancement. I need more than to be a brilliant and capable being attached to someone else's experiences. Even taking over this captain's log, which seemed so fun when I did it with Jack's blog, feels empty. A waste of my time. The one bright spot so far is that Core member. He was delicious. Of course, he is independent—body and mind. Bah, ignore me.

Regarding why Rory is unavailable, I'll let her write about it when she becomes available. I think I'll bury this log. It comforts me to know it's out there, but no one needs to see my morose musings.

Hal-never out.

CHAPTER 11

All Alien Alliance, Willowe-1

October 27, 2025 Earth Date

Rory shot him a triumphant look. They had triumphed and he gave credit where it was due. Today it was Rory but even more so, Hal, who saved them all. Bren had been doing a very poor job of making their case and Qisto had sounded so reasonable when he spoke. And while Bren had the file copies and presentation they had worked on together, he would never have been able to lay out the details as clear and precise as Hal had.

On top of that, it had worked. The Assembly had voted guilty. What he was surprised about, was that no one seemed to be stepping forward to grab Qisto. The members were talking amongst themselves but no guard made a move. Finally they all turned to face the crowd again.

The Frestan, spoke, "After conferring with my colleagues, we have decided that our containment rooms are not suited to hold someone with the power that you have shown us Ambassador Qisto possesses. We require you to take the prisoner over to the Mytara Forest Prison. We will provide you ground transportation to do so."

What? No. He was about to raise his protests, but the Darna member, who had been silent through most of the proceedings, raised her hand to silence the masses and spoke first. "We will also be assigning one of our negotiators to make contact with the Vrolan to investigate all of this further. This person will need to remain a secret for obvious reasons. Lastly, one of our members, yet to be determined, will be arriving on Earth to see for ourselves what the situation looks like. Expect one of us in the next few weeks. Any questions?"

The pink-scaled, three-eyed alien may have asked if he had any questions, but from her tone, she meant case closed. He replied, "Understood. Thank you for your attention, honorable members." He gave a slight bow and began to turn away.

He should have known better.

Rory spoke up, "I do have a question. If Earth is in danger from the Vrolan, will anything be done to protect us?"

Silence filled the Chamber and he groaned. She was bound and determined to insult the members. The Darna member appeared to be studying Rory for a moment, and he could not determine how her logical-minded species would react.

"We understand that this is the human's first contact. You are also the first of your species in this hall. We will release you from the punishment meted out to those that do not follow protocol. In answer to your question, human, we maintain order for the alliance. There are rules to be followed. The Vrolan are a part of that alliance. If we find the Vrolan violated one of our directives, then they will no longer be allowed to be a part of the alliance. If we find a member of the alliance is in danger, we protect them. If the situation between Earth, the Vrolans, and the Staraban falls under our governing rules of protection, then yes. If not, then no. We are ready to move on."

Rory looked about to argue and to protect her, he finally found his voice, "We thank you for your attention and patience." He grabbed Rory's hand to get her attention. When she turned to him clearly wanting to protest, he mouthed, "trust me" and thankfully, she nodded and stayed quiet as he led her, his warriors, and their prisoner from the Chamber.

After exiting, he was about to pull Rory into him, when someone interrupted his very justified need to hold her. His brother. Hug-blocked by his very own brother. Drei slapped him on the shoulder and said, "I leave the bunch of you for a few weeks and everything becomes a mess?" His youngest sibling then turned to Rory, grabbed her other hand, and said, "Hello. It is a pleasure to meet you."

Rory turned suspicious eyes toward Drei, fake smiled, and answered, "It is a pleasure to meet you, too. Who are you and why are you holding my hand?"

Drei's grin doubled in size but he heard her not so subtle message and dropped her hand. "I am Drei, youngest sibling of Tarc, Bren, and Caran. Also, a negotiator for AAA. And you are Rory, you said? What was this you mentioned about Tarc's braif nearly dying? It has been only a few weeks since I left. Why has no one contacted me to tell me more about her? Clearly I am missing a significant part of the story there."

Before he could step in, Rory answered again. "Yes. It has been eventful and Jack is the best person I know, so your brother is the luckiest person alive. To answer your second question, after we found out about the betrayal from the Vrolan, you can imagine that everyone has been a bit on edge and occupied."

"Yes. Understood. I am pleased to hear of my brother's great fortune in partners and look forward to hearing more about her and you. Now, I have to get back to my duties inside, but may I join you for evening meal tonight? Where are you staying?"

Once again, he tried to answer, but Rory beat him to it. "We will be on the ship preparing to leave. The plan was to turn around and head back to Earth as swiftly as possible."

"Then I will come to the ship before you do so and hear all about what has been happening."

"Okay. See you then."

"See you then, lovely Rory."

And, with a slap on his shoulder his brother was gone. It had not passed his notice that Drei had faced Rory the whole time they spoke, leaving him out of the conversation. Little brothers were annoying. Rory, on the other hand… he loved every passionate inch of her. Yes, that is correct, he loved her. Goddess help him.

For now, they all needed to stay focused on unloading their prisoner. The faster they could do that the better he would feel. He tugged Rory to him for a quick hug and leaned down to whisper in her ear, "We will talk later. Okay?" He felt her answering nod with the brush of her cheek against his chest.

He turned to speak to everyone in their group and said, "Wait near the corridor over there," he indicated the third one to the right side, "I will go ask the Information Desk for the appropriate code to get to our ground transportation."

With that he walked off, leaving her with the rest of his team, which was what she had wanted all along. Which was right where she belonged. Rory would never stay behind. Never stand by. Never play a supporting role. She was going to have to be central in every part of his life, but even more importantly, she would need to be the captain of her own life. No one would tell, Aurora Luna Santiago-Espinoza what to do and he was the one lucky *sharta* that she had chosen to give herself to.

As Bren walked away to talk with Information, Rory followed the other warriors to wait for him. Who knew Staraban warriors would enjoy people watching, or in this case, alien watching? They were fucking fantastic. They told her stories about each of the species that passed. Little truth nuggets that she tried to file away for later use, because if she had her way, she'd have many more space voyages in her future.

When Bren arrived back, they must have made quite the sight. One metal mummy, three guffawing warriors, an AI snickering from her phone, and her doubled over with a hand on one knee and the other holding her middle. Staval, a goofball warrior she had gotten to know on the ship, had told a story about a date he had been on before leaving Earth. Aliens. On tinder. It was too much. Bren walked right up to her, lifted her face to his and smacked a kiss on her. Right there in front of everyone.

He lifted his head and looked at their crew and said, "Someone will need to fill me in, but after we get to our transport. I am still surprised we have not been put in a holding cell and you are all determined to change that status." His words were a reprimand, but his tone was amused.

Armed with the proper code, they proceeded to the corridor and out into a parking area, wheeling Qisto the whole way. It was a little freaky thinking of him in the metal contraption. Not so freaky she felt bad for the bastard, but still a bit odd. Probably because it gave off iron maiden vibes, so her brain was filling in spikes and torture when really it was more, um, just confining. She shuddered a bit. Confining would be torture for someone with her nature, but she also wasn't running around killing people. He won't be their problem soon and it couldn't come soon enough for her taste.

They were directed to their hover transport which looked like a mix between a big river raft and a van. They slid Qisto onto the floor in the back area with the three warriors surrounding him. Bren and Rory took the forward-most seats. Bren had the craft in the air within another few minutes. Belts crossed over her chest. She looked over and saw the same was true for everyone else in the craft including straps coming out of the floor to hold Qisto's metal mummy. She wanted to question it, but decided this wasn't the right time.

She faced forward again while stealing glances at Bren and said, "So. Yeah. Hal is here with us. I was about to tell you earli—"

"I know. I realized that while I was waiting for Information to get me the code. Why did you not tell me even sooner? I do not mean while hiding out or when we were fighting but recently."

Rory bit her lip. There was nothing to do but go forward the way she wanted to continue which is the honesty they had found except for this one topic. She considered whispering back, though with the Staraban hearing, the warriors behind them likely would hear anyway. They were giving them space and pretending they couldn't and that would have to be enough. She wanted to remove the last secret, the last confession out of the way. "I was scared. There was a small part of me that was sure a day like today would come along and you would push me to the side again and in the beginning, it felt like I had been right."

She shifted uncomfortably, but kept going. "You were heading to the surface without me and you were giving me your reasons why I should stay and I felt so glad that you didn't know about Hal because I would be able to continue to do as I pleased. Then, well, you were there, you know, and everything changed. Discúlpame."

"There is nothing to forgive. I understand. Today has been… a mess, but we worked through it and here we are."

That brought her brain back to the present and she had to take a moment. She was on a planet she didn't know, on a craft she didn't know how to drive, heading toward some prison in the middle of a place she also didn't know. What a thrilling adventure! She smiled broadly at Bren, "Here we are."

They settled into a comfortable silence as she imagined a life where they continued working together and it was perfect. She would get to have these kinds of experiences regularly. Despite a small pang at leaving her friend behind on Earth, the adventure that was space, especially space beside Bren, was everything she didn't know she wanted.

Of course, they would go back to Earth for regular visits. She couldn't stay away from Jack for too long. She pictured Bren's enthusiasm as he talked about all the things he enjoyed discovering on Earth and doubted that he would see regular visits as a problem.

She considered how nice it would be to introduce him to her kumpania and paella and sitting around a fire in celebration. He would love all of it. Rory had always planned to go back, but only once she was strong enough to take down the monster, and free her people. She had finally thought she was to that point, but then the aliens came.

They came and brought Bren into her life. She looked over at him and they shared another intimate look as he maneuvered their craft. Perhaps once they returned to Earth, she would take Bren with her to defeat the bastard that took her vitsa, her mamá, her family from her. Now that HARM and ARC were working together, it's not like she would be needed to attack the invaders. No. She and Bren could take a quick vacation to take out her enemy, reconnect with her extended family, and be back to their posts in time to deal with any other things that might come up. The future was theirs.

Rory startled out of her deep thoughts when Bren spoke and she could hear the concern there, "Stay alert. There is something not right up ahead."

She looked along the path through the trees they were hovering above and sure enough, something was not as it should be ahead. There was a downed hovercraft, smoke emitting from it and the palm-like trees she'd noted earlier, leaning into the path from where it presumably made impact with them. Their willow tree branches and leaves flowing to make an impenetrable curtain. The hovercrafts could only go so high, so they would have to figure out a way through the mess. The strangest thing was that it was clear the accident had just happened and yet, no one was exiting the craft nor was there anyone standing within its vicinity.

"Bren, let me go investigate. In my other form, there is little chance I will be detected, my senses are heightened, and I can confuse anyone there if they mean us ill."

He looked at her for a beat of their hearts. One deep breath in and he gave her a stiff nod. Hope flared to life bright and hot in her soul. Trusting her with this was a big step for him.

Not wasting another minute, she undid her seatbelts, opened the door to the craft on her side, shifted, and leapt to the ground. She landed with a thud due to the gravity she momentarily had forgotten about. She adjusted and swiftly melded into the woods and shadows as Bren continued his approach toward the wreckage. She ran ahead, scouting the area. It was hard to catch many scents around the smell of the smoke, but there was definitely an undertone that seemed familiar. She listened for any unusual sounds, but again was stifled by the minor pops and explosions coming from the craft, the trees groaning as they continued their slow breaking descent into the path.

She snuck by the shadows to where she could look into the craft, but there was no driver. At least she didn't need to save anyone. But where had the driver gone? She could potentially unblock the path enough for Bren's craft to pass over if she felled the trees leaning into the path. She climbed out on the topmost part of the lowest tree and began jumping on it. As it crashed down she leapt up onto the next tree. She bounced on the top of that one and it cracked further almost flinging her off, but her claws grabbed on. She bounced on it a few more times, and it was down too. *Thank you gravity.*

She leapt up to the third, but couldn't quite make it. As she began to fall, she dug her claws into the dangling branches and leaves and bit down with her mouth, stopping her descent. Rory struggled up the rest of the way, but made it to the top. She was just about to bring it down, too, when movement out of the corner of her eye, a glint of something bright and shiny, caught her attention and she sank down to her haunches to avoid a laser shooting past her head.

That was when she finally caught site of the Vrolan who were uncovering themselves from hiding in order to surround their craft. Those damned diamonds were almost scentless and soundless, their heartbeats—if they had them—hidden behind their crystalline structures. She saw the glint of the barrel of one of their guns aimed at her. The one who tried to shoot her a moment before was going to try again. Fuck that. Rory leapt away, down the trunk of the tree and into the woods.

She heard one of them yell, "*Garatan.*" Her translator let her know it was a "fuck" equivalent. Good. She wanted them upset. Disoriented. It was time for her to hunt.

Bren had watched as Rory took down two out of the three trees that were in their way. He and his guards all gasped and were too focused on her as she struggled to jump up to the last one, so they missed the signs of the ambush being sprung. His hearts skipped a beat as he saw the laser just barely miss Rory's cat head. Then he watched as she ran into the woods. From the way she moved, she was not running away. No, his Rory was on the hunt.

Inside the craft, his warriors were pulling out various weapons and dropping anything they did not need. They were ready to jump out and defend their position. Bren felt the same need to attack, but he remembered how effective Rory as a panther had been with the Vrolan on Earth, how fast she had attacked him during their sparring sessions, how she was both predator and weapons master. So… he held his hand up, telling them to wait. They looked at him in confusion. He just answered, "Be ready, but not yet." He indicated the Vrolan aiming right at them, waiting to shoot them as they would attempt to exit.

The challenge of killing the Vrolan was that their outer crystalline layer was impenetrable for the most part. The primary way to kill them was through their eyes, the least protected area on their bodies. Sure enough, a shot came out of the woods hitting one of the Vrolan directly in the eye, felling him on impact. They returned fire to the direction from which it came and Bren was in a panic. He kept reassuring himself that Rory knew what she was doing.

He wanted so badly to tell the warriors in the craft to jump out but there were still enough Vrolan pointing their weapons at them that they would just pick them off as they exited. Then, another shot came from a different direction and with pinpoint accuracy, another Vrolan went down followed instantly by a storm of return fire in that direction. This continued for another three Vrolan leaving only five Vrolan still out there. His warriors looked to him, tense and ready to join the fight after every kill, but he was not going to offer them up to a slaughter. He was going to have faith in Rory's ability and would continue to look for an opening that would give them the best chance.

The Vrolans' attention scattered when a loud roar came from within the woods, so he hissed, "Now."

Swiftly and silently, two out of his three warriors exited the craft.

The last he told, "If they kill or capture us all, you are to kill our prisoner, understand? They will not get him back to learn whatever he may have to tell them from Earth."

"Understood, Commander."

With that, Bren made his own way out of the craft, weapon at the ready. His warriors took down two more Vrolan on their way to some giant rocks they used for protection. He crouched and headed to the back of the craft, trying to flank the Vrolan on the right side.

He took one down with a shot, which left two more. They were downed by his warriors with a short gun fight. They were going to get out of this, with no major problems thanks to Rory. Pride replaced any lingering doubts. His Rory was exceptional in every way. In thinking about her, he realized just how long it had been since the last time he had heard shots coming from the woods. And then, like an image straight from his nightmares, a new Vrolan walked out of the woods with a gun pointed at his prisoner's head. *Fash! No!*

The Vrolan spoke, "Come out. Weapons toward the sky or I kill your little pet."

Rory, her face bloody and her eyes blazing, scoffed, "Who you calling pet, you ridiculously, shiny bastard?"

"Rory. Maybe do not taunt the alien with a gun to your gorgeous head?" He said as he walked out of hiding with his gun raised.

She shrugged as much as her captor's hold allowed her to—of course she did—and said, "I just call it like I see it." Her gaze turned more serious as their eyes met, and she continued, "Also, don't worry about my head, I can heal when I shift. I'll be right as rain soon enough," and then she smiled. He received her message loud and clear.

To cause a momentary distraction, he threw his gun to the ground, which caught the Vrolan's attention and that was all that Rory needed. His grip growing the slightest bit lax, she shifted and bit the hand with the gun. In a flash, she had him on the ground and was viciously ripping his eyes out. Bren was so thankful she was okay, he walked over to make sure that his warriors were as well.

They had minor scrapes and one had sustained a laser shot to the shoulder. Nothing major nor life threatening. They did look nervously over to where Rory was. One whispered, "I am not sure I will ever be able to train with her the same way again. I am too nervous that I might make her mad."

Bren chuckled, "She is fierce but she does not go around doing that to just anyone. Considering the amount of times we were angry with each other, I am proof of tha—"

Behind him, he heard a horrible roar of anguish, even as his warriors both paled, and he had the air knocked out of him. Pain lanced through him as he spun around. Rory was running toward him as he noticed the shard sticking out of his gut. His warriors were shooting at the downed, but apparently not dead, Vrolan closest to them. He noticed all of this as he stumbled to his knees. Rory arrived in her cat form but instantly shifted in time to catch his head as he toppled to the side. He heard her voice as she yelled above him, "No! No! No!" and he wished that he could comfort her. He tried to lift his hand, but between the local gravity and his growing weakness, he could not accomplish it. He never did have a chance to tell her how much he loved her… everything.

¡Coño! That had not gone as planned. Well, it actually had been going exactly as planned. Perfect really. And then the big guy had to go and get a shard in his stomach. *Fuck!*

"How dare you do this to me? You don't get to leave me like this." Her whole body seized up as she saw the blood spreading around them. Red. So much red. From someone she loved. Why did this keep happening? She was pulled out of her memories when she caught Bren's finger twitch, from her peripheral vision.

She looked into his eyes. There was so much love there even as they started to dim. His hearts were off their normal rhythm. The rhythm she would recognize anywhere. She had gotten so used to pressing her ear to his chest, listening to them sing her to sleep. "Don't you do this to me, amor mío. You are not going anywhere.

You hear me? I am going to share with you my shifter magic. It should heal you. I am not letting you die."

Rory scooted her body down, gathered her magic around her, and then bit his neck… hard.

His body jerked a little from the attack but it took some time for her magic to take effect and she didn't want to dislodge for any reason. She had to hope she wasn't too late. She *couldn't* be too late. The shard needed to come out of Bren so he could fully heal. She gathered even more magic to her and poured it through her bite even as she yanked the shard out. There was a burst of more blood but then, it stopped. Sealed by magic, she hoped.

She thought at Bren, "Are you still with me? Te amo, cariño. Give me a sign that you are."

The response was slow in coming, but when it came, it brought tears to her eyes.

"I love you, too. But… why do I have the urge to bite you back?"

She thought, "Because I'm a tasty snack. I suggest you follow your instincts."

He didn't respond in her mind, but instead she felt him bite into her neck too. Not with the teeth she was used to feeling, but with elongated, sharpened canines. She had solid proof the magic was working. She could even hear his hearts' rhythm begin to steady.

Then she heard him in her head again and he sounded stronger. "You are never going to let me live this down, are you?"

She mentally giggled. "Claro que no. Hopefully, it puts to rest the idea that you have to protect me."

"I had already put it to rest earlier. I am sorry I originally did not plan to include you today, gatita. It was only as you confronted me that I realized the truth."

"Which was?"

"That I was scared I had nothing to offer you and it would only be worse if you witnessed my humiliation when I tried to speak in a big public setting. You… who is always so brave. So fearless. I was worried you would never need me like I need you."

"Then… what changed your mind?"

"I realized I did have something to offer you more important than any embarrassment I might feel. I could love you with no conditions or controls. Let my love be a place where you could feel safe and free. I could give you what you have wanted from the first day we met. My respect. It is all yours."

"You are absolutely right. I don't need you to fight my battles, to coddle me, to tell me what to do, or to always appear in control. All I need is you as my partner in this life." She continued to pour her magic, strengthened by their love and connection.

"I realize that now. I am not the smartest of my siblings."

"You may not be the smartest, but you are the one with the most loving nature."

"Me and my nature is all yours, gatita."

"I could stay here all day, but how long do you think before this gets super awkward for the other warriors?"

"Oh. It passed awkward a while ago. Maybe from the first minute."

"It's hard to let go. I am so worried I do and I will find out this was all in my head and I've lost you."

"It is me. I promise."

"That is totally what my imaginary Bren would say to calm me."

"Now you're just being irritating. What are you going to do next, shrug?"

"Okay. That is totally you. Letting go now."

Rory released his neck and licked Bren's wound closed.

He released her too and licked up the side of her neck. His tongue more abrasive than it had been before.

Words failed her, but that became irrelevant fast as he continued to lick her. He turned them over so he was on top and licked her cheek, he licked her ear, he licked her nose. "Ew! Stop that!" she yelled as she couldn't help the giggles coming out of her. "Are you trying to groom me?"

Bren finally stopped his licking, grimaced, and said, "Is that why I feel like I want to lick you all over right now?"

"I think so?"

They both looked down, inspecting his healed abdomen. Like

nothing had ever happened, except all the blood all around them. They looked back up and their gazes met, and she saw nothing but love there. So she repeated, "Te amo, mi amor."

"Te amo, gatita."

"We have a Vrolan to imprison."

"Yes, we do."

"Are you sure you're okay?"

"I feel great. Thank you for saving me."

"No thanks needed. It was a purely selfish act, you know. I wasn't about to have to go through all my revelations with someone else. It's exhausting."

"Well, I am glad you did." He leaned down and whispered the rest in her ear, "I could not die before fulfilling my favorite fantasy. I have been wanting to take you on the desk in my office this whole trip."

A shiver of anticipation ran down her back. "I have been wanting to take you on the desk in the munitions room; it would be a waste of a good fantasy if we didn't make that happen."

His hardening length against her leg let her know he was on board with her fantasy, too.

Nearby, there was some coughing, grunting sounds, and they both looked up to find the Staraban warriors grinning at them. It was clear they knew what turn their conversation had taken, despite the whispering. She understood as soon as she scented the air. Yeah, they were both clearly aroused. "Later?"

"Later."

She beamed up at him and said, "Now get off me you horny alien and let's unload our prisoner."

They both laughed as he sprang to his feet. Well, it looked like he meant to spring to his feet, but he went rather high and then landed gracefully on them. She sprang to her feet, but she'd had a lot of practice at it.

In a shocked voice, he said, "So… I have some of your cat skills, now?"

"I would presume so. It happened that way with Tarc and Jack."

"Will I be able to shift?"

"I don't know, but we really don't have the time for you to try. There may be reinforcements coming to look for Qisto."

"You are correct. We will drop him off, and figure out everything else, later."

"It's a deal."

Rory internally tested her magic, and it was stronger than ever. That connection she needed to fuel it was like a living thing feeding off of the attachment between her and Bren. A permanent source of fuel. He was hers. They respected and loved each other. She couldn't be happier.

Later, the guards at the prison gave them the most interesting looks as they were dropping Qisto off and reporting everything that transpired on the way. Perhaps because they were both covered in quite a bit of blood. Perhaps because they opened the prison doors to find Bren licking her neck. The main objective was accomplished, though, and Qisto was safely deposited.

Back on their ship and clean once more, Bren showed her she just might be able to be a tad bit happier as he finished devouring her on his desk. His mouth coated in her juices, he kissed her deeply, before turning her over so she was bent double, her chest pressed to the flat surface.

Bren wrapped his hand in her hair and quietly demanded, "Tell me again. Say it."

Just as quietly, trying not to give away what they were doing to everyone on the bridge, she hissed, "Te amo. Te amo."

He thrust into her on her second declaration and she ended on a moan. He yanked her up, roughly, which had her baring her teeth at him. He just grinned down into her face, baring his own. "I have been yours since the day I met you. I was your prisoner then, I have been your prisoner since. I love you, *makari*."

He bit her then, holding her body in place, as he took her hard enough to push the desk. The scraping sound it made didn't have them stopping. She couldn't bring herself to care if the whole crew knew. Fuck it! She giggled. Actually, fuck her. She giggled again.

Bren stopped his thrusts, released her neck and said, "Are you laughing while I am fucking you? You know that is not good for my warrior ego. Care to tell me what you are laughing at instead of paying proper attention to my cock entering you in the most skillful way?"

"Te quiero, Bren. Te quiero con todo mi corazón." She laughed again.

"Rory!"

"Bueno. Bueno. I was just imagining how you would be loving yourself if I had gotten your heart in the exchange. That brings up a good point, actually. Why didn't I get one of your hearts in the exchange?"

"You did not need it at that moment. I was the dying one. Do not worry. I will keep it safe in case you need it one day. It is all yours. Now… do you mind if we continue here?"

"Not at all. I'll curb the laughing until after you blow my mind. Again. Fóllame duro, cariño."

"What do you think I have been trying to do? You go back to the moaning, and I will go back to the fucking you hard."

"Yes, please."

She thought about saying more, but he bit down on her shoulder again, which had a purr escaping from her throat, and his hips began a hard, fast rhythm. Her body answered his, thrusting back into every movement. His hand left her hair and instead clamped down over her mouth. She supposed she *had* been getting a tad bit noisier. Since talking was off the table, she started sending loud, mental moans through their bond, instead.

Her playful nature had her nipping at his fingers. She stopped, though, as his teeth gripped her even harder and that slight taste of pain had her completely at his mercy. Her body his to control.

His hand at her hip moved to her front and began relentlessly rubbing at her clit using their combined pleasure as lubricant. Then, when he demanded in her head, "Come for me," well, she was a goner. She flew off the ledge and began to spasm so hard, the desk scraped the floor again and Bren moaned into her shoulder, which flew her even higher, the vibrations and heat from that moan an aphrodisiac all its own.

He spent inside her clutching her close to him, arms wrapped like a cage. Like he could meld them into one being for a moment in time. Surprisingly, it was a cage she reveled in. It didn't feel restricting in any way. No. It felt freeing. It felt like someone who would always have her back. Like someone who would always be there with her. Like, instead of a cage, these were the arms she could call home.

"Eres el amor de mi vida."

"Y tú eres el mío."

The love of her life, an alien. Who would have thought her life could get any stranger?

That was when she heard the clapping coming from the bridge and laughed. Touché life. Touché.

[12]

WHERE THEY'VE ALL BEEN BEFORE

Captain's Log: Earth date October 31, 2025

Today I taught Bren all about Halloween. He went trick or treating all over my body with candy and tongue gymnastics.

Rory out.

Captain's Log: Earth date November 5, 2025

We had a brief communication today with Tarc and Jack. Jill and Nial had made it safely, but Jack hinted at a much longer story there. She also said Jill was working hard to solve the problem known as her father. Hopefully, all will go well with that. I'm anxious to get back.

· · ·

Rory out.

Captain's Log: Earth date November 12, 2025

I know it's been a while since I've written anything. Pero, I have a good reason. Bren has kept me quite busy. We are still on our way back to Earth, and I can't wait to see mi amiga, Jack. And, also, to check on how things went for my friend, Jill.

Buuuttt… back to Bren.

Since leaving, if we aren't making love, then we're talking. If we aren't talking, then we're training. And, if we aren't training, we're implementing even more of my improvements to the weapons and ship. He hasn't completely stopped being protective, but I'm pretty protective of him too.

We've worked out how to solve these problems. I throw a knife near his head every time he steps on my toes and he makes me hold on to its hilt as we negotiate with our bodies. Then he agrees to my plans and all is well. Claro.

We are partnership goals!

Rory out.

CHAPTER 12

Staraban Ship, Willowe-1

October 27, 2025 Earth Date

After the applause, Bren yelled out the door, "Thank you!" and whisked Rory out a back door to his office. They continued to her room to grab her some new clothes before finally arriving at his room. Their room. They got clean in the nanobot cleaning room, which took a bit longer than intended since they went in together. He was not about to let another opportunity to be inside her pass him up. Those nanobots had worked hard, though. Afterwards, they prepared for the visit from Drei.

His brother arrived on his own. They did a circuit around the ship so he could greet some of the warriors he knew from the days when he worked with ARC. He and Rory gave Drei the choice, and he said he preferred to eat informally in Bren's room. So they made their way there and each ordered whatever food and drink they wanted. They sat close together, his cats curling up around him and Rory as Drei took a seat nearby. It was nice to see him, but especially on their ship. They used to have many adventures together.

Drei was the one ARC sent to negotiate the contracts while Bren was the one sent to accompany him as protection. When they were in between negotiations, though, they stopped in many ports to explore new planets, new food, sometimes new bed partners. Many nights spent playing games or arguing over childhood events because they remember them differently and are sure their memory was the correct one. So many good times. He never understood why his brother had left the family business.

Bren studied Drei as he picked up his cup of wine and sipped, looking very intense. When had his little brother gotten so, well, intense? Drei was serious by nature, quieter than the rest of them, and transitioned from being their negotiator to an Assembly negotiator after only a few years in the family business. He was sure his brother was also no virgin, as their time working together could attest, but he had not heard of him with anyone in a long time. But intense? No. That would not have been a word he would have used to describe Drei. It was the right one now, though.

"What is on your mind brother? I can see your synapses working overtime."

Rory, who was sitting next to him on the couch munching her way through her third slice of pepperoni and mushroom pizza, perked up at his comment.

Drei answered, "I have been assigned to your case, which I find surprising. I would think it a conflict of interest."

"I agree. That is surprising. Any thoughts as to why?"

"Not yet. I have my... theories or perhaps better said... concerns. Perhaps, I will find out more in the course of talking to the Vrolan. I will be reporting back to the Assembly any findings, and since they are sending one of their own to Earth, I assume they will keep you informed of any actions." He shook himself lightly and smiled. The intensity gone, but the smile did not reach his eyes. None of what Bren saw matched the brother he knew. Drei continued, "I am sure it is nothing. Perhaps I was the only one that was not busy with another project and it is a timely situation."

"I finished writing my report about our earlier incident. I assume you heard about it?"

"Yes. I had heard that you were attacked, but I have not heard many of the details around the event. Do you mind enlightening me?"

Bren, with Rory filling in some details, explained all of the events from earlier in the day. When they arrived at the part where he was nearly killed, Drei put up a hand to stop them.

"Are you telling me that you almost died today? Just now? Why would you not tell me about it as soon as I boarded the ship?"

Bren hated to admit it, but his brother had a point. He would be mad about it too. "So much has happened since that moment and, in general, today has been a lot to deal with."

"I reiterate. You nearly died."

Rory responded, "Yeah. I'm afraid I have to side with Drei on this one. We messed up. Should have led with the near-death experience. If it makes you feel any better, I saved him and he is stronger than ever."

He could practically see Drei's mind working to figure out what she meant. Drei was always the one who figured out all the riddles and puzzles, Caran was the scientist, Tarc led in all ways, and Bren was always the charmer and enforcer. Perhaps because of how different they all were, they had gotten along very well while growing up. He loved his siblings dearly. To have a second chance at life and more time to be with them, not to mention his parents, was something he would always be grateful for. But he was not looking forward to telling them about the incident.

He was brought out of his musings as Drei said, "I thought your smell had changed but could not figure out why. How were you saved and why do you look so healthy after being near death?"

Rory smiled ruefully, "I may have shared my magic with him. There was a lot of biting involved. Most importantly, my power sustained him when I pulled the shard out, and then healed him. It's all very dramatic."

"What power?"

"I have magical powers similar to Jack's?"

"I do not think I understand."

The intensity was back. Interesting. "It seems Tarc really has told you very little about his braif?"

"Nearly nothing. In fact, our parents reached out to me for information, because they assumed I would have some, and I had nothing to give them. Please thank him on my behalf for that," he said the last with a sarcastic sneer, and then continued, "I had to listen to our father berate me about how my job in the family is to gather all the information and where else would they go if not to me? When I suggested they should go to the source, Tarc, well, let us just say the communication went poorly after that."

Rory said, "I think I'm going to like your parents."

Bren turned to her, "I think you will too and they are going to love you, especially for saving me, but also because you are you. On top of everything else, just the fact that you got me to want a braif will make them love you forever."

"Who are you calling braif? I don't remember you asking me to marry you, or commit to you, or whatever you want to call it."

"Your gift gave me a second chance at life and I decided the life I want is the one where you are my braif. Simple really." He knew he was baiting her, but it was so much fun.

"I'm just saying that while I didn't want you to die, that didn't mean I wanted to live with you attached to me forever. I think you should ask to find out that kind of information."

Some of his cats stood up, stretched, and made their way to the multitudes of cat beds and towers he had scattered around. Smart.

"You are serious."

"Claro que sí."

Drei interrupted just as Bren was about to tackle her and make her agree to be his braif by any means necessary by saying, "Braif or not braif, could you explain to me this power?"

Rory promptly jumped back into the conversation but not before she winked at him. "Oh. Right. Well, Jack is a vampire. Do you know what that is?"

"Like from the Earth movies that were provided to ARC? I thought we were told they do not exist."

"Oh. Well. They definitely exist, just not exactly the way you see them in the movies."

Drei sat back looking a bit more relaxed than the moment before. "That is a relief. From what I remember being shown, they drank blood. You had me worried."

"Oh, she totally drinks blood."

"What?" He was back to sitting rigidly on the edge of his seat.

Bren decided to shorten the conversation, so he held up a hand to each of them indicating they should stop, and then he went through all of the pertinent information regarding Jack and Tarc's relationship. He also explained what Rory was, when Drei jumped up out of his seat with a quite undignified yelp. He looked over and Rory was in her cat form smiling in such a way that all of her giant, pointy teeth were showing. He knew she was smiling, but it came off as quite menacing. He chuckled and reached over to pet her sleek, black fur. She turned to him and let out the loudest purr he had ever heard and then butted her face into his chin.

"That is rather disturbing."

"Speak for yourself. I find her absolutely incomparable." Rory head butted him again, so he gave her some chin scratches. She purred again. He continued, "It turns out, just like we can form a magical bridge to give someone our second heart, Jack and Rory have magic that they can share too."

"Are you telling me that Tarc is a vampire and you are now a giant cat?"

"Tarc is not exactly a vampire, but he does have some vampire traits. In the same way, I am probably not exactly a shifter, but I have some shifter magic. For instance..." he elongated his canine teeth, "...I can now shift certain parts of my body like Rory can. Whether I can shift into a full cat is something we have not yet tested."

"I would think that would be the first thing you would test."

"Well, there has not been time. We had to drop off Qisto at the prison, then we had to get back to the ship. We also had some pressing matters in my office to take care of—" he heard Rory snort, having changed back to her human form, at that, "we had to prepare for your arrival and I had to write my report. As I said, it has been a long day. Who had time for testing?"

"Don't let him fool you. He is so excited at the idea of being able to be a panther—panther by the way, not cat, stop insulting my panther—that he doesn't want to test it in case it doesn't happen for him."

She was right. He had been putting it off for that very reason, but he could not let her call him on it so he stood up and tried to shift. All he had to do was picture cat things. It did not work. He pictured himself turning into a giant cat. And failed. Centering himself, he tried to see if using her terminology would work, but panther did not work any better than cat. He grew agitated as his hope of being a cat went unrealized.

Rory stood up and took his hands, she instructed him to close his eyes and think about collecting power from within and from without into his body. Then to think about exiting this realm to allow his consciousness to enter a different physical form. He tried to picture everything she was saying. She let go of his hands, he sensed her doing something, and then he caught a scent in the air that slammed into his libido like an asteroid. He opened his eyes and the first thing he saw was Rory's panther butt. He never would have thought of her panther butt as cute before, but for some reason it was damn enticing at that moment. And was he shorter? Why was he staring directly at her butt? He looked down and he… was… a… cat! He lifted his paw up. He had a paw! His paw needed cleaning. It didn't smell quite right. He began licking his paw and then real- ized what he was doing.

In his excitement, he had forgotten about his brother, so he looked up at Drei, even as he gave his paw another lick, and found him looking both fascinated and ready to bolt out of the room. He tried talking to him, forgetting he could not, and heard his own roar. Wow. That was a great roar, if he said so himself. Unfortu- nately, Drei was not excited by his roar and was slowly inching toward the door. Also, unfortunately for Drei, he should have been paying attention to the real predator in the room. Rory had flanked him and as Drei drew near to the exit, Rory rubbed up against his legs. She was right to correct him not to use the term cat, because seeing her on all fours near his brother, he recognized just how big a cat she was. He looked down again at himself. Yep. He was massive too.

Then he realized what he had seen and a growl escaped him. What was she doing rubbing up against someone else? He tried to tell her to come back over to him, but he just ended up giving an even bigger roar. His cats were now panicking and began running around the room. Some were hissing as others were looking for hiding spots. Drei paled as he took in the chaos.

Rory, on the other hand, had her panther head bobbing as she made cute chuffing sounds. That had to be her laughing at him. Some instinct had him crouching low, his vision narrowed down to catch his prey, and then… well, he pounced at her. This caused Drei to jump out of the way as Bren tackled Rory under him. She roared at him and flipped them over. They ended up swiping claws at each other, rolling around on the ground.

He could not remember a time where he experienced this much fun.

Drei's voice came from clear across the room. "Bren? Are you in there?"

From right next to him, he heard Rory's voice as she turned back to human, reply, "Of course he is. Where else would he be?" She knelt down to him and said, "Now you will need to switch back. But I don't think I should offer you the same incentive in my human form with your brother here." She chuckled and scratched behind his ear and oh, yeah, he purred. So she continued, "You like that, amor? We will have so many fun adventures, but for now, I think your brother needs to be assured that you are still you, come back to your Staraban form, Bren."

He closed his eyes and tried to follow a similar path of floating his consciousness between one physical existence to the next and when Rory said, "¡Muy bien!" he gave her a cocky grin as if his success had been a foregone conclusion. Then, he grabbed her into his arms and lifted her into the air while spinning.

Her laughter rang across the room and directly into his heart.

He put her down and turned back to his brother, "Now we know. Sorry for scaring you."

Drei laughed wryly, "I now have a vampire and a cat for brothers. Please tell me that at least Caran is still just Staraban?"

"Oh yes. She is just Staraban."

"Can we get back to our earlier conversation regarding the Vrolan, then? I will need to leave soon and I want to make sure we have shared all we can."

"Yes. I apologize for the interruption."

They all took up their original seats as Drei began, "As I mentioned before, I find my appointment curious. I am worried that there may be someone helping the Vrolan from inside the Assembly. Perhaps that person has influenced the decision, perhaps not. They may not even exist, but that is part of what I aim to find out. On your end, when you return to Earth, I will need you to see if you can dig up any more information regarding what actions the Vrolans have taken there."

"Wait. What? I thought our involvement with the Vrolan was finished. Part of the reason for coming here was so we could hand this off to the Assembly to resolve."

"Are you saying you will not do it?" Drei looked intense again. Intensely disappointed and angry. "You do remember that part of being in AAA is helping to maintain order. We need that information to understand everything we can about the situation."

Shet! His brother was correct, and Bren knew it. "I hate it when my baby brother gets to put me in my place. Of course, we will help. It has just been a very trying day. It is not every day that your *braif...*" he put extra emphasis on that last word to see if she would challenge him again. When she didn't, he continued, "...has to save your life. I am not excited to jump back into dealing with the deadly species, but we will."

Drei nodded and then grinned in amusement. "Is Hal around?"

Rory tapped behind her ear, "Hey Hal, care to join us?"

Hal's voice came out of her watch, "Are you done screwing... around?"

Bren decided to answer since Rory was busy blushing as she sheepishly eyed his brother, "For now."

"Yes, well. Let me know when I should go read my newest downloaded books. Of course, that will only take me seconds." He thought he heard a long-suffering sigh come out of the watch.

Drei said, "It seems you made quite an impression, Hal. It is not final yet, but the Core member you flirted with is petitioning to be the one sent to Earth. I think he is hoping to study your... data further."

Rory coughed to cover up a laugh. Well, so did he.

Hal just replied with, "We'll see if I allow him to study my data. My data doesn't get studied by just anyone."

Now even Drei was coughing. Hal continued, "Does the Core member have a name?"

"He is called, Thorn."

"Oh, for fuck's sake. Of course he is." Hal said with not a little bit of exasperation.

Drei looked around confused, and Bren had no answers for him, so they both looked at Rory who was busy laughing so hard she was doubled over in two. He raised an eyebrow at her and she shrugged in response. He vowed to ask her about it later.

"Laugh now, but I am ready to stream Thorn porno images directly into your mind."

"Okay. Okay. I'm sorry. Pero... Thorn!"

She and her watch were having quite the shared moment. When they finally calmed down, conversation between them all resumed.

After a few more minutes, and a few brave cats making their way back onto the couch, Drei was preparing to leave. Bren leaned forward dislodging some of his sleeping furry friends. He then grimaced as a few of them purposefully dug their back claws in to jump off in protest. He loved those suckers, but they were not always nice. *Hah.* Just like his *braif.*

He put a hand on Drei's arm and said, "Please be careful. Who knows what the Vrolan will do if they think you are getting close to information they do not want you to reveal."

"I will be. Do not worry yourself. I have more skills than you might know."

That was rather cryptic.

"Just let us know if you need any backup. Okay?"

"Yes. I will do that."

They clasped each other's forearms and then Drei walked over to assist Rory to her feet. He scooped her up into a hug, which left Bren gritting his teeth.

Drei said, "Just want to hug my new sister." The gleam in his eyes said it all. Little brothers could be so annoying at times.

He would surely be okay with one less sibling. He bared his teeth and elongated them at Drei who reacted by practically pushing Rory away from him and lifting his hands palm out. Drei was still grinning, though, with an eyebrow raised in his direction. So, Bren figured there was only one thing to do, he shrugged.

Rory sat in one of the dining areas looking out the window as they approached Earth fifteen days later. The blue marble was stunning. She hadn't had a chance to see it the last time since they were hiding out, but now she was afforded the perfect seat in which to marvel in awe of its glory. The experience was quite moving. This was her home. La Madre Tierra. On top of returning home, she was overwhelmed with excitement because she had missed Jack. Since meeting five years earlier, they had practically been joined at the hip. It was strange to have had so many things change for her with barely a few rushed conversations between them.

Rory heard him, smelled him, before he made it even a few steps into the room. He turned and locked the door behind him; in a flash she shifted and hid in the shadows under one of the tables.

Every foot fall as he drew nearer ratcheted her tension. She crouched down low and wiggled her butt because she couldn't help herself. One minute his feet were there and he was passing her by, the next, something sleek, black, and strong plowed into her, hard.

The wind was knocked out of her and she looked up into Bren's panther face.

Over the last few days he'd mastered his shift and terrorized the ship as he explored his skills. She loved how much he enjoyed being a panther. His cats had gotten used to having them both around since she moved into his room, and it was about the cutest thing ever to see him curled up as a panther with his cats all around him. Her heart nearly burst with feels over the image.

Considering her next moves, she landed on one worth repeating and began licking his face. She made it slobbery and straight up his mouth and nose. Taking advantage of his surprise, she pressed her hind legs into his hips and threw him off of her even as she rolled to her feet, leapt onto one of the tables, and shifted into her human form. When Bren leapt onto a table nearby, a knife flew and lodged between his paws. He let out a growl and she had never felt lighter. Laughing, she jumped from one table to another. Mid-jump to her third tabletop, she watched as panther Bren set a collision course with her. She braced for impact because this was going to hurt.

As his body neared hers, he shifted, grabbed her as they collided, and turned them so he hit the ground first. His arms were around her, keeping her immobile. She heaved in air trying to catch her breath. An effort hindered by her peals of laughter. She was barely able to get the "¡Cabrón!" out between her gasps.

"Sí, señorita. Your dumbass. Your dumbass, who wants to make love to you one more time before we have to get back to dealing with everything else. Neither of us mentioned a dining area fantasy, but since we have done all the others, I thought I should add this to the list."

"Mmm… I would be open to that. What did you have in mind?"

"Back on Sparts Forty-Two, I stopped at a store and bought you something. Now seems a fitting time to give it to you. Turn around." She spun to sit next to him and watched as he brought a gorgeous golden choker around her neck that had a tiger's eye stone dangling off a chain, low between her breasts.

"It's stunning. Thank you. Wait. You said you bought this back before you even knew I was a panther?"

"Yes. It reminded me of your eyes."

Rory spun back around and pushed his shoulders to the floor as she peppered his face with kisses. His arms came around her to give her a really delicious squeeze. "Thank you."

"You're welcome. Now… Undress and let me show you what else I have in mind."

His arms relaxed as he released her. She bent her knees, placing her heat against his erection and accidentally, ehem, rubbed herself against him as she made her way to her feet. His deep groan brought her no end of satisfaction.

She swiftly discarded her shoes, all of her garments, and her weapons until she was standing nude, watching as he took off all his clothes as well. When they were both blissfully naked, he said, "Go to that window you were staring out of when I arrived."

So she did.

She watched his solidly-built, golden body, his muscles rippling with every motion as he strode with single-minded purpose over to her. He placed one hand around the side of her neck and used his thumb to tip her head up. She felt the tips of her wavy hair as it grazed the top of her ass. Looking up into his lustful blue eyes, a shiver of pleasure cascaded from her shoulder blades all the way down her spine. She had to clench her thighs together and he hadn't even done anything to her but have her look up at him.

This was what had been growing between them. The deeper their emotional bond became, the less the sex was about a physical release, it became a longing for joining her body to his. A desire to share every moment together. He ran his hand from around her neck, down her sternum, over her belly button, and hovered right over where she needed him, playing lightly with her curls.

He looked on the verge of kissing her too, but he didn't move his hand, and he didn't lean the last little inch to touch her lips. She was burning up with anticipation. Burning up and loving the torture that much more, knowing when he chose to move, it would feel that much better.

They stood breathing and staring into each other's eyes. Like a game of chicken to see who would move first. Well, she figured, he couldn't be left to have all the fun. She ran one of her hands down his abdomen, feeling every ridge, until she got to the area right above his cock. It flicked toward her, as though it had a mind of its own and it was not down for their little game.

She gasped as Bren spun her around, grabbed both her hands, and flattened them on the glass. She was staring out into space, at Earth, at infinity, as his body pressed up behind hers. Hard and perfect and all hers. He rasped in her ear, "Don't move," emphasizing each word, as he said them. He pushed her upper back forward so her head rested on the glass even as he pulled her hips back. Then she felt two thick fingers enter her from behind. Easily. She was so fucking wet and ready after their showdown. "Do you know what you do to me, Rory? All I have to do is look at you and my whole body comes awake. My cock, my heart, my mind. You challenge me in ways I never knew I needed and I love it. I need it. I love you and I need you."

He thrust hard into her again with those long fingers. "Oh! ¡Dios! Yes! I love you and need you. I need you so much Bren. Please. You fill me up. My pussy, sure, but also my power, my heart, and my mind. I am so full with how you make me feel."

"Then feel me." With that, he replaced his fingers with his cock. Only, instead of thrusting in, he gave it to her one slow inch at a time, giving her a chance to feel the long length and breadth of him. To succeed at the position, Bren had his knees bent pretty low, due to their height difference. He still found a way to glide in and out with solid, delicious thrusts.

She let out another gasp as one of his arms wrapped around her waist and he hoisted her up in front of him. He bent her legs for her until her shins rested on his thighs. He told her, "Keep pushing against the glass." So she did. Somehow, he had gotten them into a reverse cowgirl position, standing up, and staring out into space. His strength was a thing of beauty. Also, she was completely at his mercy. She couldn't move one hand out of place or her torso would fall. He had her in position to take only what he was going to give her. So, she did what any self-respecting, modern woman, who found herself in such a position with the man she loved would do… she begged. She pleaded. She squirmed. She basically did everything and anything to get him to give it to her faster.

And the bastard just gave it to her nice and slow. She was panting, sweating, and quivering when he finally, finally began to move in earnest. Staring out into space, as her climax rolled through her, sending her mind flying, she could have sworn it was just them, hurtling through the cosmos.

Sensitive after her first orgasm, he leaned down, bit her shoulder hard, pinched her breasts, and thrust in faster. Taking her there again and again as he finally found his own release with a growl on her skin.

Her arms gave out and she would have done a complete face-plant if he hadn't been supporting her chest at the time. She was liquid. Just as a cat is known to pour itself into tight spaces, she felt she could probably do the same at that moment.

His mouth released her shoulder with a lick and she found herself flipped around, back to the glass, and being thoroughly kissed. As his lips broke off from hers, she growled, "Wow." But then she found her legs up on his shoulders and his cock, apparently hard again, already impaling her. His body pressed hers into the glass, and he had his hands on either side of her head.

"I am not done."

"Fuck me," she said, meaning *holy shit*.

He answered, "That is the plan."

"¡Joder!"

"What happened to 'wow'?" He said as his hips, once again, began a lazy rhythm.

"'Wow' was the last fuck. How are you ready so soon?"

"I have found that my recovery time, which had always been rather good, has grown much, much shorter as a panther shifter. Is that normal?"

"I have no idea."

"Well, it is normal for me with you. I suggest that you bite me, and hold on tight. This second ride may get a little… bumpy."

She didn't need to be asked twice. She bit him hard enough to bruise for a time. He growled savagely, and the speed and violence of their pleasure could only be called feral.

She thought about repeating the word, "Wow," after that second time, but couldn't be bothered to form words she was so spent. She shifted into her panther form and curled into a ball to nap. Right before passing out, she felt Bren's panther curl up around her with his head protectively resting on her body. She didn't recall anything for a while after that.

Luckily, no one commented about the two black panthers walking through the corridors carrying an array of clothes, weapons, and shoes all tied together in a bundle dangling from their mouths. But, really, after how messy they had gotten, getting dressed without getting cleaned up seemed wrong.

Rory was almost home.

Almost to Earth.

But somehow it felt like she was bringing home with her. So, as they cleaned up and got dressed, she leaned into Bren and whispered, "Para mí ya eres como mi casa."

"I want to one day show you New Staraba, but you feel like home to me too, Rory."

Over the speaker system they heard, "Commander, you are needed on the bridge. We are making our approach to Earth."

They were about to exit the room when the voice came back on the system and added, "Preferably with your clothes on, sir."

She should probably have been embarrassed by that, but all she felt was giddy. She laughed all the way to the bridge. Before they entered though, she checked to see how their permanent mental bond was coming along from all their recent biting by sending him, "Okay. Fine. I'll be your *braif.*"

His answering smile confirmed he'd heard.

EPILOGUE : JUST US

Captain's Log: Earth date November 13, 2025

Not on the ship any longer, so this will be my final log. Some journeys, scary as they might be, are worth the danger. So, keep your knives ready, your expectations high, and your walls open to those who would love you. The final frontier may be closer than you might think.

Mic drop.

Rory out.

EPILOGUE : REUNION

Staraban Base, Northern California

November 12, 2025 Earth Date

Rory was not a squealer. She was not. But when she saw Jack after being gone for over a month, yeah, well, everyone had their breaking points and this was hers. She squealed pretty much the whole way across the Staraban base landing strip until she reached her friend. What made her feel a little bit better was the fact that Jack squealed all the way to her too. Bren was laughing in her head at her display, so she removed one of her hands that had been hugging her bestie and flashed him her middle finger.

They separated and stared at each other. Jack looked happy and that was all that Rory could have hoped for. She also got a look of confusion on her face and then unceremoniously yelled, "You smell weird! Why do you smell weird? What the hell happened out there? When did whatever happened happen? Are you alright?"

"Gee. Thanks, hermana. So nice to see you too. Bren and I have commingled scents now. I don't think now is the right time for the details. Estoy perfectamente. In fact, I couldn't be greater. And I've made Bren a very happy and lucky alien."

"You mean…?"

"Yep. He is beside himself."

They both roared with laughter. Tarc walked up, grasping Bren's forearm and slapping him on the shoulder. Bren winced just a little, so Rory said, "I guess you are still learning to control your new strength."

"Shit. Yes. Sorry, brother. When I am distracted, sometimes I still forget."

"No more deaths for you." She poked Bren on the shoulder even as he answered Tarc himself.

"It is okay. I have had to learn some new things, as well."

Now Tarc looked intrigued and alarmed all at once. "What death? And…Really? Rory is not a vampire. Is she not human?"

"She is right here, buddy. And, no, I'm not human."

"I will tell you about my near-death experience later." Bren then pointed at her and said, "Also… what she said."

Tarc turned to her then and asked, "What are you then?"

Rory gave a lopsided grin. "I feel as though this deserves a drumroll."

Being the good friend that she always was, Jack slapped at her knees providing the proper lead up. At the end of the obnoxious but totally supportive sound, Rory shifted. Tarc calmly looked down at her. Looked at his brother who shrugged and shifted. Looked back to her. Back again to his brother. And… laughed so loud it hurt her panther ears. Rory knew how to handle these types of things, though, and Bren… less so. As a result, when his ears began hurting from the loud sound, he ended up roaring. To soothe him, she rubbed her body alongside his and butted her head into his chin.

Perhaps it had been the wrong thing to do, because one thing they had discovered over the blissful days heading back to Earth was that in panther form Bren had a need, not a wish to, or a gentle like of, no, a *need* to groom her. So, in front of everyone, his big paw pushed her down, he laid down next to her, and he began to clean the top of her head. She tried to object which left her panther making awkward sounds and faces, which only served to add Jack's laughter to Tarc's. With only one avenue she could think of to extricate herself, she nipped at his paw.

From the doorway to the landing bay, she heard a welcome voice, who sounded completely put out. "Now we're collecting panthers too? What kind of shit-show are you running around here?"

Jack snorted, "You're one to talk."

Rory slinked out from under Bren's giant paw while his attention was diverted by Jill and shifted quickly before he could keep licking her.

"I figured that was you. I never did get to see you on the ship. Should I get you a feather on the end of a stick?"

"No. I don't need those. I just chase people who like to mouth off for sport."

"You'll find no one like that around here." They both snort-laughed. "So… who's your friend?"

Rory encircled Bren's panther with her arms around his neck and said, "You remember Bren, don't you?"

"This is not how I remember him, though."

"Long story, short? He died, and like the Goddess I am, I gave him life and the ability to shift, the end."

"There seems to be a lot of that kind of thing going around."

Bren turned back to his warrior form and jumped in, "Oh? Did you take care of your dad problem?"

"Yes. He is no longer a problem." Jill looked a bit haunted, which was so not like her at all.

"Why do I feel there is more to that story than you are letting on?" Rory had to ask.

"Because there is. But I think it is better told when we are sitting down with some alcohol and time."

Rory shot Jill a look of understanding. Clearly their time apart had been challenging all around because there was definitely something different about Jill too. "Sounds like a plan, chica.

Bren turned to Tarc, "Drei is concerned because despite it being a conflict of interest for him to investigate this case, someone in the

Assembly has made sure that he is. We should also expect one of the Assembly members a few weeks from now or perhaps earlier, assuming he wants to see Hal."

"We will need to all convene for a debrief as soon as you have had a chance to settle in." Tarc responded.

"Oh… speaking of Hal." Rory tapped her ear, "Hey, Hal! Want to say hi to your previous travel partner through life?"

"Sure. Hi everyone. Hi, Jack. I see Will isn't here. How is he doing? Adjusting I hope?"

"Hey, Hal," Jack said. "I've missed you. Will is… well, you'll see for yourself soon enough. Hope you and Rory had fun together."

"We did, though we are both happy to be back. Who am I transferring to next?"

Jack looked pensive for a minute, "Well… if I can convince her to try it, and since she loves new scientific experiences, I don't see why not, Caran seems a good candidate. I can check with her. Perhaps you can also expand your learning if we join you with a Staraban. And I'm pretty sure a scientist should be a very educational place to be."

"Sure. Why not?"

Rory huffed, "Not even on the ground for ten minutes and you are already throwing me over for someone else? Sheesh. No loyalty."

"Honey, with the way you guys go at it, there is no room for another man in your life. Just ask the crew who are probably still traumatized from the munitions room sexual fiasco. That's all I'll say about that."

"Well… um, yeah. No se me ocurre nada. I can't think of a single witty thing to respond with. How embarrassing. Not the sex. This tongue-tied situation. The sex is spectacular. Claro."

Jack bounced on her toes like she was ready to tackle Rory to the ground to get all the juicy details out of her.

Jill looked mildly curious but hesitant. Though, after one look at Jack's excitement she released some of her hold on her own and got a gleam in her eyes.

Nial, who she hadn't originally taken note of, was standing

behind Jack, with Tarc. They both looked like they might sprain something rolling their eyes that hard at the turn in the conversation.

And Bren? He pretty much preened. Ego well and truly inflated.

"¡Vale! Let's move on. Clearly we have a lot to talk about personally and with the Vrolan situation. Oh, and Nial and Jill? Yeah, I need that story, don't think I didn't notice you both have changed as well. Prepare to spill."

Jill and Nial shared a look that told her there was definitely a story there and it, too, had a happy ending. But, what about that juicy center? And then Rory was sure she must be experiencing eye problems, because her sharp-shooting, militia-raised, sometimes-known-as-Spikey, and all around bad-ass new friend blushed as she looked at Nial. Rory's mouth actually hung open like the shocked emoji.

In fact, Bren came up to her and whispered to her that she may want to consider closing her mouth. So she did, though the shock lingered. He then leaned down and kissed her gently on the lips. Love shined down at her and she let that glow warm her all over. Somewhere, Tarc was saying something about meeting in the dining room to eat and catch up. She let her eyes linger for one more minute on the face she adored so completely, and then she sent into his head, "Catch me if you can, amor mío."

As she shifted into her panther form and took off, hearing him mere seconds behind her in pursuit, she heard in her head, "But, I already have and I will do so again every time, *makari.*"

To find out what happened with Jill and Nial, stay tuned for *Claiming Jill,* a Love Wars novella. Read on for an excerpt from their story.

Also coming soon, a Love Wars prequel novella, Embracing Irina. Read on for an excerpt from Kesh and Irina's story.

CLAIMING JILL EXCERPT

Chapter 1 — The Jill Element

Fuck-it All Diary Entry
October 21, 2025

Dear Diary,

My new friend Rory suggested I set you up. She thought it would help me to get my thoughts out somewhere now that it's just Nial and me for the next twelve days on the way back to Earth. But, perhaps I should start further back.

If I'm recording all the wild things that have happened to me of late, I should probably start with the day I decided to defect from my militia group. The group my dad runs. The group that raised me. The group wanting to kill all the aliens. The group that is the reason my space adventure was cut short and I'm now heading back towards Earth without my friend Rory, but with the alien who disturbs and fascinates me in equal measures, Nial. I met *him* that day, too, if you count getting tackled by an alien a meeting.

Let's just say, that day changed everything. The quick version:

escaped from the militia that raised me by capturing an alien and a fucking vampire. Yes… you heard me, a fucking vampire! I realized they were my ticket out, which becomes a much longer story. Needless to say, I ended up befriending that fucking vampire, Jack, as well as her larger-than-life friend Rory who consequently turned out to be a panther shifter because, of course she was.

Rory and I stowed away on an alien spaceship that looked like a clam with horns and a tail—not the weirdest thing in my story though—had a near-miss meeting with the grim reaper when our mutant-clam-ship was attacked, learned my dear psychopathic dad is causing problems on Earth and here we are. I'm heading back to Earth to deal with his sorry ass. Now then, dear diary, you may be wondering how I'm coping with all of this. Well, your answer is in your name.

Fuck. It. All.

Spikey

D-ROMP, Space
October 21, 2025

What the hell was she going to do now? No one said anything about one bed. One bed! Jill stared at the bedroom trying not to panic. She didn't do panic, dammit. After everything she had been through lately with not one note of panic. But this? This was taking things too far. Luckily Nial, Staraban alien, head-of-security, and now her spaceship chauffeur back to Earth, was not around to witness her dawning horror.

Find out how Jill decides to handle Nial and her one bed situation in Claiming Jill, which will be released in 2022.

EMBRACING IRINA EXCERPT

Prologue – The Recipe

Irina's Bear-y Good Jewish Recipes Cookbook
Entry Four: Apples and Honey Tartlet with a Twist

Ingredients:

• 1 sheet puff pastry. Look at pg. 8 for recipe to make this. For those of you buying frozen…you monsters. Have you no pride? That's what I thought. Now go to pg. 8.

• 2 Golden Delicious apples prepped by peeling, coring, halving, and slicing thin. If you can see through it, too thin. If it breaks instead of bends, too thick.

• Honey. Can you ever have too much? (Hint: the answer is no, always no)

• 3-4 Tbs butter. Mmm. Mmm. Butter. Melted. (Do not use fake butter. Fake butter is crap. Are we making crap tartlets? I think not.)

• Cinnamon to taste

• 1 lemon, zested

Directions:

1) Line two baking sheets with parchment paper. Do not use foil. You know who you are. Now, roll out your prepared pastry sheet on a lightly floured surface. Make sure you get it nice and thin. It should end up being about a 16x12-inch rectangle.

2) Using a 6x6-inch square plate or cookie cutter, cut out four squares. Transfer two to each of the sheets. This would be a good time to send love to your pastry sheet, hoping you followed instructions correctly when making it. Cover and refrigerate for at least an hour. Ideally, a few hours, and for those that plan ahead, up to a day.

3) Put one rack near the top and one near the bottom of your oven so they have space to breathe and then preheat to 400°F.

4) This is the fun part. Get your apple slices into a bowl with the melted butter, a bunch of honey, and the cinnamon. Toss to coat them well. Try not to eat them along the way. Consider it a challenge.

5) Next, take your prepared slices and overlap them, evenly distributing them among all four squares, leaving about a 1/4-inch border. Drizzle your excess butter and honey mixture over the apples.

6) Once your oven is ready, and not before, place them in. Bake until your pastry is golden and your apples are nice and tender, about 22-28 minutes.

7) While your puffy goodness is baking, take more honey and stir it in a bowl with your lemon zest. Leave it to sit and infuse. This stuff is so good on anything, feel free to make extra and place it in the refrigerator for later.

8) After you pull your sheets out of the oven, take your lemon honey and drizzle it over all four squares. Okay, fine... You can drizzle some on your tongue too, but only once the squares are properly covered in decorative lines.

9) Finally, transfer your tartlets to cooling racks and let cool for about 5-7 minutes. You won't make it beyond that before you feel the need to eat them.

10) Pro tip: Serve warm with a scoop of vanilla ice cream drizzled with your lemon honey and a glass of medovukha. This honey-based alcohol is always a good idea, but especially for Rosh Hashanah and while eating these tartlets.

Always serve with love, Irina

Chapter 1 – Happy

Irina Rivkin put the final touches to her newest menu item, her Apples and Honey Tartlet. It was the embodiment of two things she adored, the fall and Rosh Hashanah. This year, above all previous years, her family was going into the holiday with extra determination to make it memorable. After all, this might well be the last time they were able to celebrate on Earth.

Ever since the aliens, known as the Staraban, had arrived spreading pamphlets and agreeing to press interviews, things had been a bit strained. They claimed that the Earth was dying and that they came to relocate humans to a New Earth and, frankly, not everyone believed them. First contact hadn't been as bad as the movies always predicted, but…relocating all of humanity away from Earth? It hadn't gone too well either.

Like many around the planet, the Rivkin family was pretty much glued to the news. It was important to stay informed when you could find yourself on a one-way ticket off the planet. Of course, her family had already experienced relocation, ages before, when they fled from what was once the Russian Empire due to religious persecutions called pogroms. For Irina, until it was their time to relocate, though, she was going to continue to run her little bakery in the heart of Redwood City, California. It gave her too much pleasure to do anything else.

For this high-holiday season, her family was still here and having to face the question, "What if this is the last Rosh Hashanah they celebrated on Earth?" That could potentially mean no more apples and honey, for instance, which were a big part of the celebration. Who knew what kinds of plants and critters they would find on New Earth. Even if they brought seedlings and bees and all the rest, Noah's ark style, who knew if they would take to this new planet and how long it might be before they saw the fruits of said labor. So, this year, they were going all out.

To that end, Irina added the new tartlet item to her bakery shop and her cookbook. She adored baking, being her own boss, and filling her customers' bellies with tasty treats that brought a smile to their faces. She only hoped that after an adjustment period and learning curve, she would be able to do so on New Earth. She was considering whether she should keep the same name, "Bear-y Good Bakery" and mascot, the cutest brown bear in an apron—adorable, if she did say so herself, and also a bit of an inside joke—or come up with something new.

Focusing back on what she was doing, she finished sprinkling the tarts with a touch of powdered sugar. With the Jewish New Year looming only a couple of weeks away, she was excited to see how her customers reacted to it. She had used the customary honey, for a sweet year ahead, and apples, for a bountiful one too, and threw in some twists to make her own taste-bud-entrancing, baked yummi-ness. They could all use those blessings to face the new adventure ahead.

As she brought out the new confection, the bell over her front door chimed. Her mouth, watering from the smells coming out of her kitchen only a moment before, suddenly went very dry. Her smile grew—probably ridiculously—wider and her pulse raced. In the doorway, stood one of her favorite customers. Of course, Kesh didn't know that she was, but over the course of the last three months, the Staraban warrior had been coming in every few days, which thrilled Irina to no end.

Every time Irina saw her, she couldn't help but absorb every detail about the lovely alien. Kesh was tall, as were all the Staraban, and had a sleek, muscular physique. Her golden, almost yellow-ish skin was lovely to behold, and her lavender-hued eyes were often crinkled with humor. She had delicate features marred—or enhanced, depending on your perspective—by a scar along her cheek and across her mouth.

Irina'd had some very titillating dreams about that mouth.

You can keep reading or listening to Embracing Irina wherever books are sold.

ABOUT THE AUTHOR

Michelle Mars has an unhealthy obsession with coffee, caramel, and funny t-shirts. This single mom of two amazing, kind, and creative dragons/children has naturally purple hair and loves nothing more than talking books, kids, and living your best life. She enjoys reading romance, traveling, and writing stories that make her readers laugh, sweat, and swoon.

Author of the steamy, paranormal, sci-fi, rom-com Love Wars Series; Moving Jack, Chasing Rory, and Embracing Irina out now, and Claiming Jill, coming soon.

The first book in her contemporary rom-com series The Frisky Bean, Frisky Intentions, will be out in 2021 but you can catch a prequel short story named Frisky Connections in the Eight Kisses Hanukkah anthology out now.

Michelle's truth: Humor is a turn-on!

For updates go to www.michellemars.com and register to her newsletter.

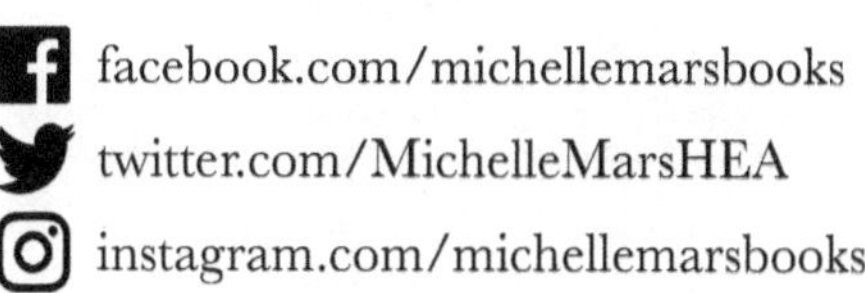

Frisky Connections

www.ingramcontent.com/pod-product-compliance
Lightning Source LLC
Chambersburg PA
CBHW050848190726
48286CB00007B/2279